BLUECOAT AMBUSH

Touch the Sky spotted it first.

A brief glint of military brass, emerging from the opening of that coulee on their left. And even as he spotted it, his newly emerging shaman's sense told him it was too late.

Only a heartbeat after Touch the Sky made the discovery, Little Horse too spotted the officer.

"Brother, leap!"

But it was too late to jump out of the way. Even as Carlson pressured the last fraction of trigger resistance, Little Horse lunged off his pony and into the path of his friend.

Touch the Sky felt his face drain cold when, with a sound like taut rawhide bursting, the bullet struck Little Horse in the chest.

The *Cheyenne* Series:

8 CHEYENNE
WAR PARTY
JUDD COLE

LEISURE BOOKS　　**L**　　**NEW YORK CITY**

A LEISURE BOOK®

December 1993

Published by

Dorchester Publishing Co., Inc.
276 Fifth Avenue
New York, NY 10001

Printed in the United States of America.

Prologue

In 1840, when the new spring grass was well up, a Northern Cheyenne named Running Antelope led his wife, infant son, and 30 braves on a journey to counsel with their Southern Cheyenne kin living below the Platte River.

Running Antelope was a peace leader, not a war chief, and his band rode under a white flag. Nor had they painted or dressed for battle, nor made the all-important sacrifices to the sacred Medicine Arrows. Nonetheless, they were forced to fight when blue-bloused pony soldiers attacked them in a pincers movement near the North Platte.

It was the Cheyenne way to flee during battle until a pursuing enemy's horses faltered. Then the Cheyenne would suddenly turn and attack. But a hard winter had left their ponies weak. Nor were their stone-tipped lances, fire-hardened arrows, and one-shot muzzle-loaders any match for the Bluecoats' percussion-cap carbines and big-thundering wagon guns that shot scream-ing steel.

Still, the braves fought the glorious fight, shout-ing their shrill war cry even as they sang their death song. When flying canister shot cut down their ponies, they used them for breastworks and fought on. But eventually Running Antelope, his squaw, and all 30 braves lay dead or dying. The only survivor was Running Antelope's infant son, still clutched in the fallen chief's arms.

Pawnee scouts were about to kill the child when the lieutenant in charge interfered. He had the baby brought back to Fort Bates near the river-bend settlement of Bighorn Falls in the Wyoming Territory. John Hanchon and his barren young wife Sarah, owners of the town's mercantile store, adopted the child. His Shaiyena name lost forever, he was raised as Matthew Hanchon.

His parents were good to him, and at first the youth felt accepted in his limited world. He worked for the Hanchons, earning hostile stares and remarks from some customers, but also making friends in Bighorn Falls. Then came his sixteenth year, when tragedy struck his safe little world.

Matthew fell in love with Kristen, daugh-ter of the wealthy rancher Hiram Steele—the Hanchons' most important customer after Fort Bates itself. Caught in their secret meeting place, Matthew was severely thrashed by one of Steele's hired hands. And Steele warned Matthew: Stay away from Kristen or he was a dead man.

Afraid for Matthew's life, Kristen lied and told him she never wanted to see him again. But even then the youth's misery was not complete. Seth Carlson, a jealous cavalry officer with hopes of marrying Kristen, issued an ultimatum: Either Matthew left Bighorn Falls for good, or Carlson would use his influence to ruin the Hanchons' mercantile contract with Fort Bates.

Saddened, but determined to know if the tribe of his birth would accept him, Matthew fled north to the up-country of the Powder River—Cheyenne hunting grounds. Captured by braves from Chief Yellow Bear's tribe, he was declared a spy for the hair-faced soldiers and sentenced to death. But at the last moment Arrow Keeper, the tribal shaman, interfered and ordered the prisoner freed.

Arrow Keeper had just returned from a fateful vision quest at sacred Medicine Lake. His epic vision promised the arrival of a mysterious Cheyenne youth—one who carried the mark of the warrior on his body. And one who would eventually lead the entire Shaiyena nation in one last, great victory against their enemies. For despite the prisoner's white man's clothing and language, Arrow Keeper had spotted a mulberry-colored birthmark buried well past his hairline: a birthmark in the perfect shape of an arrowhead, the mark of the warrior.

Arrow Keeper insisted that the youth must be allowed to live with Yellow Bear's tribe, to train as a warrior. His white name was buried forever, and the tall youth was given the Indian name Touch the Sky.

This infuriated those who wanted him executed as a spy. These included Black Elk, the fierce young war leader who hoped to marry Chief Yellow Bear's daughter, Honey Eater. Black Elk noticed the glances Honey Eater gave this handsome stranger. And early on, Black Elk's younger cousin, Wolf Who Hunts Smiling, stepped between Touch the Sky and the camp fire, thus announcing his intention of killing the white man's dog.

From the beginning of his training, Touch the Sky faced many trials and much suffering in his quest for acceptance in the Cheyenne world: He helped to save his tribe from destruction by Pawnees and white whiskey traders and land-grabbers; he fought against Crow Crazy Dogs, Comanches, and bloodthirsty Kiowas. But throughout all of this, the hatred and jealousy and mistrust of his tribal enemies only strengthened.

Now Black Elk, hard but fair at first, has finally succumbed to jealous rage over Honey Eater. Touch the Sky's recent rescue of Honey Eater, when she was a prisoner of Kiowa and Comanche slave traders, has further humiliated Black Elk in the eyes of his fellow warriors. And Wolf Who Hunts Smiling, realizing that Touch the Sky is the main obstacle to his ambitions for tribal leadership, has vowed to eliminate this obstacle once and for all.

Chapter One

"Brother," the young warrior called Little Horse said, "a thing troubles me greatly. I would speak with you about it."

Touch the Sky glanced up from the new bow he was fashioning out of green oak. He sat in front of the elkskin entrance flap of his tipi. Their sister the sun had already gone to her resting place, and now Uncle Moon owned the sky. A fire burned in a circle of stones. Orange spear tips of flame illuminated Touch the Sky's strong, hawk nose, pronounced cheekbones, and long, loose black locks. Though he was seated, it was clear that he was tall and broad-shouldered, even for a Cheyenne.

"You know I always have ears for your words," Touch the Sky told his best friend in the tribe. "Sit and speak of this thing."

Little Horse had brought his favorite clay pipe,

filled with kinnikinnick—a mixture of coarse tobacco and fragrant red-willow bark. He sat beside his friend and lit the pipe with a piece of glowing punk pulled from the fire. Little Horse was much smaller than his friend, but built strong and sturdy like a good war pony. Unlike Touch the Sky, he wore his hair wrapped tight in a single braid, the style preferred by men of his clan.

As was the custom, the two young braves did not immediately broach the subject on Little Horse's mind. Instead, they smoked for several minutes, speaking of insignificant things and watching the camp come to life as darkness descended.

There was no established "bedtime" in the Cheyenne village, now located in the lush grass at the fork where the Powder River joined the Little Powder. Often the camp stayed lively and loud all night long. Braves placed bets on pony races and wrestling matches; children played at taking scalps and counting coups; sad old grandmothers keened in grief for sons and husbands whose bones had been strewn on battlefields from the Missouri River to the Marias.

Finally Little Horse set the pipe between them, the sign that he was ready to begin talking.

"Brother, you are no white-livered Indian. I have fought beside you when you waded into battle fighting as fierce as a she-grizzly protecting her cubs. You have defeated many enemies, as the scalps dangling from your coup stick prove. But sometimes the most dangerous enemies live closest to home. Even the fierce badger has been killed in his own burrow."

Touch the Sky met his friend's eyes but said nothing, only listening. Beyond the well-lit circles of the clan fires, a coyote raised its ululating howl to the heavens, a howl that ended in a series of yipping barks. The tall young brave knew full well what his friend was hinting at.

"Black Elk has always been covered with hard bark," Little Horse said. "But there was a time when he tried to be fair to you. That time has long passed, thanks to his jealous rage over Honey Eater. Now, since you saved her from the Kiowas and Comanches down south in Blanco Canyon, the other braves in his Bull Whip Society goad him on. They tell him, 'This Touch the Sky, he wants to put on the old moccasin with your squaw!' "

Touch the Sky nodded, watching sparks float up from the flames like fireflies. "Putting on the old moccasin" was a reference to a young, unmarried brave who was eager to rut with a married woman.

"I fear greatly for Honey Eater's safety," Touch the Sky admitted. "Black Elk has already cut off her braid to shame her, and he has beaten her. Now, since he failed to rescue her, he threatens to kill her if she so much as looks at me."

"You speak straight-arrow. But buck, it is not only Black Elk you must watch. His young cousin is enraged since the Council of Forty punished him. Wolf Who Hunts Smiling hates you as never before—I have heard warnings from

Tangle Hair and other Bowstring soldiers friendly to you.

"Wolf Who Hunts Smiling now speaks in a bark against you every chance he finds. He tells the younger warriors you are a white man's dog. That because palefaces raised you, you have the stink of the whites on you for life. He has made it the mission of his life to destroy your name within the tribe."

Again Touch the Sky could only let silence acknowledge the truth of these words. During a recent buffalo hunt far to the southwest, Wolf Who Hunts Smiling had served as a hunt soldier: one of the braves who enforced the strict Hunt Law which governed buffalo hunts. Using his authority to arrest, he had falsely accused Touch the Sky of illegally employing a buffalo jump— driving part of the herd over a blind cliff to their death, a serious violation of Hunt Law permitted only if horses were not available.

But Wolf Who Hunts Smiling was not content with the severe whipping this false accusation earned Touch the Sky. He went on to bribe an old squaw of the Root Eaters Clan. He convinced the addled old grandmother—known for her prophetic medicine dreams—that she had experienced a "vision" concerning Touch the Sky. She then announced, before the entire tribe, that the youth must set up a pole or else his white man's stink would ruin the hunt.

Tribal belief in such medicine dreams was strong, Touch the Sky had no choice but to undergo the grueling penance. Bone hooks were driven into his breasts, and he was suspended for hours from a pole atop a hill. But later, Arrow Keeper discovered Wolf Who Hunts Smiling's treachery and reported it to Chief Gray Thunder.

Recently, by a formal vote of the clan headmen comprising the Council of Forty, Wolf Who Hunts Smiling had been stripped of all his coup feathers—a serious blow to a haughty, proud warrior who constantly boasted of his battle prowess. Now there were no white eagle-tail feathers in his war bonnet. Now admirers could not count how many times he had defeated his enemies.

Even as Touch the Sky was about to answer his friend, three shadowy forms passed near the edge of his fire.

"Steady, Cheyenne," Little Horse said in a hushed tone. "Here come your enemies now, traveling like curs in a pack."

Touch the Sky recognized Black Elk, Black Elk's younger cousin Wolf Who Hunts Smiling, and a brave from the Wolverine Clan named Swift Canoe. Swift Canoe had played the dog for Wolf Who Hunts Smiling and wrongly accused Touch the Sky of killing his twin brother, True Son.

The trio stopped, their stern faces outlined in the flickering flames. Black Elk was the oldest. He looked especially fierce because of the dead, leathery flap of skin where one ear had been severed in battle, then crudely sewn back on with buckskin thread. Like the others, he wore a soft kid breechclout, buckskin leggings, and beaded elkskin moccasins. A small rawhide medicine bag dangled from his clout. It held a set of lethally sharp panther claws—the special totem of his Panther clan.

"Look here, stout bucks!" Black Elk called out to his companions. "Here sit two of the white men's favorite spies, plotting new ways to play the big Indian while they sell tribe secrets to hair-mouths!"

"Indeed, cousin, I smell the stink of whites all over Woman Face," Wolf Who Hunts Smiling said. He was smaller than Black Elk, and younger, but his strength and agility were fearsome. His dark, furtive eyes constantly moved like minnows, missing nothing.

Touch the Sky said nothing at the allusion to "Woman Face," refusing to rise to such familiar bait. This was a mocking reference to his former habit of permitting his feelings to show in his face—a white man's trait despised by Indians as unmanly.

"Even the buffalo run from this stink," Black Elk said.

"But the red men have run from it long enough," Wolf Who Hunts Smiling added. The young brave had looked on, horrified, when a burst of Bluecoat canister shot turned his father into stew meat. Now tight anger sizzled behind every word. "It is time to feed all the white men and their dogs to the carrion birds."

It was Little Horse who next spoke up.

"You three speak of white men's dogs until I am weary of hearing it. The first scalps to dangle from *our* clouts were those of hair-faced whites."

14

"So you say," Black Elk replied. "But you yourself saw *this* one"—he pointed at Touch the Sky—"drinking strong water with hair-faces at the trading post. Both of you were seen holding secret council with blue-bloused soldier chiefs, and leaving talking papers for them in the forks of trees."

"During a bad flood, a snake will share a dry rock with a rat. This does not make them lodge brothers. What is seen and what is true are not always the same."

"Hold, brother," Touch the Sky said, gripping his friend's shoulder. "Do not waste time arguing with words. Words are the coins spent freely by old squaws. These talking magpies are nothing. Men let their war lances speak for them."

"*Men,*" Black Elk said, "find their own wives instead of holding another man's in their blanket."

"No man can steal that which is his by right," Touch the Sky replied.

Absolute silence greeted this remark. All four braves clearly understood Touch the Sky's point. Despite having undergone the squaw-taking ceremony with Black Elk, Honey Eater's heart belonged to Touch the Sky alone. Only her mistaken belief that he had deserted her and his tribe had led her to accept Black Elk's bride price. And then only because tribal law forbade her living alone after Chief Yellow Bear, her father, had crossed over.

Black Elk's fierce dark eyes glowed with the hatred of blood-lust. His hand moved to the bone-handled knife in the beaded sheath on his sash. Wolf Who Hunts Smiling and Swift Canoe followed suit.

As one, Touch the Sky and Little Horse rose to meet the attack.

"I will not stain the sacred Arrows by being the first to let Cheyenne blood," Touch the Sky said. "But close against me or Little Horse, and I will leave your warm guts steaming on the ground."

"Cousin, I for one am weary of this bloodless sparring," Wolf Who Hunts Smiling said, moving a step closer. "This make-believe Cheyenne would rut with your squaw! I say we make maggot fodder of him now!"

Cheyenne village life centered around a huge clearing, in the center of which was a hide-covered council lodge. On a lone hummock at the river edge of the clearing stood the tipi of old Arrow Keeper, the tribe shaman and keeper of the sacred Medicine Arrows. A pony with markings unfamiliar to Gray Thunder's camp was hobbled before the tipi.

Inside, a fire blazed in the stone-lined pit in the middle of the tipi. The buffalo-hide tipi cover was almost stretched transparent with age, and was now transformed into a dull-orange cone by the fire within. Old Arrow Keeper sat across the fire from a young Cheyenne brave named Goes Ahead.

Goes Ahead was a word-bringer who had ridden south from the camp of the Cheyenne Chief Shoots Left Handed. It was located far to the north in the mountains near the Land of the Grandmother—the land called Canada by the whites.

"Now, little brother," the old medicine man said after they had smoked to the four directions of the wind, "unburden your heart to me and speak straight-arrow. I can see, from the trouble clouds in your eyes, that the news from my old friend Shoots Left Handed is not good."

"Not good, Father, not good at all. Trouble has infected our band like the red speckled cough. I do not even know if the rest will be alive when I return."

These somber words deepened the sharp creases of the old shaman's face. He already knew the situation must be bleak indeed—Shoots Left Handed had instructed this word-bringer to go directly to Arrow Keeper, not Chief Gray Thunder or the headmen. This suggested there was no time for the usual, lengthy proceedings of a council.

"What is this trouble, little brother, that places such a weight of age and sadness over your young face?"

"Our band has been blamed for several attacks on white stagecoaches and freight wagons. Pale-face passengers have been wounded, goods and money stolen. White settlers in the region have blood in their eyes against the Shaiyena people. Now we live on the run, driven higher and higher into unfamiliar mountains."

Arrow Keeper's brow creased in a puzzled frown. "Southern Cheyenne Dog Soldiers sometimes raid this way. But no Indian loves peace more than Shoots Left Handed. Surely no Cheyenne from his band would do this thing?"

"None, Father. We are certain of this, yet we are blamed."

"But little brother, the area where you live is crawling with Blackfeet, not Cheyennes. Everyone knows Blackfeet attack whites at every opportunity. Why, then, are Cheyennes being blamed?"

Goes Ahead shook his head. "No one understands this thing. Soldiers and vigilantes come for us in the night. We move our camp often now. But our meat racks are empty and game is scarce in the high country where we are forced to hide. There is no grass for our ponies, the children and elders are sick, pregnant squaws are losing their babies. Worse yet, we have little strong medicine to fight back since Scalp Cane was killed."

Both Cheyennes automatically made the cut-off sign, as one did when speaking of the dead. Now Arrow Keeper was deeply troubled. Scalp Cane gone, crossed over! For more winters than Arrow Keeper could recall, Scalp Cane had served as medicine man for Shoots Left Handed's band. How could a tribe face trouble such as this without strong medicine? Indeed, perhaps the loss of Scalp Cane's big magic was behind the current trouble.

And perhaps, Arrow Keeper told himself, the hand of Maiyun, the Good Supernatural, was in this thing.

Old Arrow Keeper thought again, as he did often lately, about his young apprentice, Touch the Sky. The tall youth's existence with the tribe had proven difficult since that first day, many winters gone now, when he had been captured, taken before the Council of Forty, and pronounced a spy for the hair-faces.

However, recent events had endangered Touch the Sky more than ever before. It was as clear as blood in new snow that Black Elk's jealousy over Honey Eater had finally driven him insane with suspicion and rage. And being stripped of his coup feathers had left the mean-spirited Wolf Who Hunts Smiling keen to punish his enemy. Either brave would gladly sully the sacred Medicine Arrows—and thus the entire tribe—by killing Touch the Sky.

The old brave had been thinking, even before Goes Ahead rode into camp, that perhaps it was time, once again, to send Touch the Sky away for his own safety. For one thing, despite Touch the Sky's youth, Arrow Keeper knew his medicine was strong. He also knew the youth possessed the gift of visions. What better Cheyenne than he to send north to help Shoots Left Handed, whose people had no spiritual guide through this difficult time?

Besides, Arrow Keeper had intended to eventually send the youth north anyway. The elder had experienced a powerful vision at Medicine Lake. One which told him that Touch the Sky must be prepared for eventual leadership of the entire Shaiyena nation. He must meet their northern allies and familiarize himself with the land of the short white days.

"Wait here, little brother," Arrow Keeper said,

rising with a popping of stiff kneecaps. "I must speak with someone."

His mind a riot of troubled thoughts, Arrow Keeper headed across the central camp clearing toward Touch the Sky's tipi. He pulled up short when he viewed the tense scene which awaited him. Touch the Sky and Little Horse stood shoulder to shoulder in front of Touch the Sky's tipi. Facing them, hands on their knives, were Black Elk, Wolf Who Hunts Smiling, and Swift Canoe.

"Cousin, I for one am weary of this bloodless sparring," Wolf Who Hunts Smiling was saying, moving a step closer. "This make-believe Cheyenne would rut with your squaw! I say we make maggot fodder of him now!"

There was a quicksilver glint in the firelight when Wolf Who Hunts Smiling slid the polished obsidian blade of his knife from its sheath. His companions too drew their weapons.

"Then close the gap!" Touch the Sky said, his knife leaping into his fist. Little Horse too drew his blade. "I am *for* you!"

"Hold! I command it in the name of the Arrows!"

Arrow Keeper's voice was cracked and old, but carried the stern authority of age and wisdom. All five braves stared at him. One glance at the scene had convinced Arrow Keeper that his decision to send Touch the Sky north was the right one.

"You three," he said, his hatchet-sharp profile directed at Black Elk and his companions. "Return to your clan circles!"

War Party

But Wolf Who Hunts Smiling's blood was up to kill this white man's Indian who had cost him his coup feathers. More and more he had been openly challenging Arrow Keeper's authority.

"This old one has grown doting in his frosted years!" he said scornfully. "His brain is soft with age."

Black Elk, however, recalled the many times that Arrow Keeper's medicine had blessed his war bonnet and shield.

"Cease this unmanly disrespect, cousin, and do as your Cheyenne elder commanded! In good time we will settle with Woman Face."

After they had left, Arrow Keeper turned to Touch the Sky and Little Horse.

"You two. Ready your battle rigs and equip yourselves for a long ride. But keep your preparations secret. I want *no one* in the tribe to know that I have sent you north on a dangerous mission."

Chapter Two

The Milk River Stage and Freighting Line operated the only stagecoach service between the Bear Paw Mountains of northern Montana and Fort Buford in the remote Dakota Territory.

The desolate stretch between Fort Randall and Birch Coulee was especially treacherous. In the higher elevations, rock slides occasionally wiped out the wagon road; below on the plains, sudden downpours could mire the wheels up to the axles in minutes. There was also the constant threat of Indian attack.

Jeanette Lofley knew all of this very well because her husband, Colonel Orrin Lofley, was the commanding officer at lonely Fort Randall. He had finally agreed, reluctantly, to send for her despite the considerable dangers of the long journey in this far-north country. The War Department had recently notified him he was being kept at Fort Randall for another two years. Upon learning this, Jeanette told him bluntly she would rather be a widow than an Army wife. It was she who'd insisted on her leaving Michigan to join him.

But now, watching the seamed bottom of a steep canyon slide by just a few feet to the right of their narrow, twisting trail, she missed the placid shores of Lake Erie.

She was a pretty, dark-haired woman of perhaps 30, her pale and serious face still unlined. She shared the six-passenger coach with a portly, bald-headed major named Carmichael— an administrative officer returning to Fort Randall after temporary duty in the Dakota region— and two civilian cattlemen headed for the railroad spur at Milk River.

"We're nosing into the rough stretch now," said one of the cattlemen, a lanky, rawboned man named Legget. "This next twenty miles is where the last two attacks took place."

"What gripes me," said Starret, his companion, "is how the Army buckles under to the Indian lovers in Congress. They just sit back and let the redskins rule the roost hereabouts. Blackfeet, Mandans, now Cheyennes. My wranglers know this north country. They ain't too eager to push beef through it. I have to double their wages once we cross the Yellowstone."

The officer named Carmichael frowned. "It's no use to blame the Army. You can blame that goddamned—excuse me, ma'am—you can blame the Fort Laramie Treaty. *That's* what ties the Army's hands hereabouts. According to that treaty, whites are to punish white criminals, Indians are to punish Indian criminals. The Army has no legal jurisdiction against aboriginals on the road through Indian country. That's why Colonel Lofley can't even send out a detachment to protect his own wife."

"Blamed fool treaty," Legget said.

"I'll grant that, sir. The Army doesn't like it either. You can thank the Quakers back East for it, what with all their Noble Red Man and brotherly love claptrap."

"What's that?" Starret said, craning his neck out the window on his side.

Legget paled a bit, then stuck his head out too. "Where?"

Starret caught Jeanette's eye and winked. "Oh, I reckon it's just a stand of trees. I thought maybe it was a group of Indians."

Starret chuckled as his friend frowned and shot him a disgusted look. "Don't be playing the larks with me like that, Jim. It ain't funny."

"Well anyway," Carmichael said, again letting his gaze fall to the creamy white skin at the neck of Jeanette's shirtwaist. "Even if the colonel couldn't provide a detachment of guards, he did the next best thing. The man riding shotgun is named Jay Maddox, and he's a sharpshooter from Fort Randall. He can shatter a shaving mirror at five hundred yards, shooting over his shoulder."

Jeanette gripped the pleated leather armrest as the stage shifted to climb a steep incline. She heard the steady jangle of the traces, the driver cursing the team and lashing them with his light sisal whip. The coach was equipped with iron springs and leather braces, but still jolted and bounced roughly on the rock-strewn trail. Behind, the boot was stuffed with luggage. Overhead, the iron-reinforced security box was lashed tight to the roof. It contained a gold shipment bound for the huge trading post at Pike's Fork.

By standing agreement, the only people who knew when such shipments were coming were the traders at Pike's Fork, Colonel Lofley and his immediate staff, and the men at the stage line. Despite recent Indian attacks, it was generally believed that red men this far north had no concept yet of the value of gold. The colonel had explained all this carefully to Jeanette. But still she glanced nervously to right and left, suspicious of every cloud shadow or hidden gulch.

"No need to fret, ma'am," Major Carmichael said deferentially, taking her slim white hand between his own pudgy fists to pat it reassuringly. "Young Corporal Maddox is the pride of the Army. And as you can see, I'm armed too. You're well protected."

Legget opened his linsey suitcoat to reveal a six-shot pin-fire revolver in a leather holster over his right hip.

"Made for me special-order in Philadelphia," he boasted. "There's a fold-away knife blade under the barrel. You can—"

"What the hell?" Starret said, his face stiffening with fear as he stared toward the rimrock overhead.

"Jim," Legget said, "Don't wear it out. I like your barroom josh as well as the next fellow. But there's a lady with us now, and you—"

Jeanette watched Starret flinch violently. A moment later she heard an insignificant little popping sound. Not until Starret flopped back in his seat, a neat hole in the middle of his forehead, did she realize the popping sound was gunfire arriving a heartbeat after the slug's impact.

"Good God a-gorry!" Legget said, even as a geyser of blood spurted from his friend's forehead and splashed Legget's coat.

"Hi-ya! Hiii-ya!"

Hearing the fierce, shrill cries from without, Major Carmichael shouted, "That's the Cheyenne war cry! Christ on a crutch, we're being attacked by Cheyennes!"

Now it was clear to all that the Indians had picked a perfect place to attack from above. The stagecoach was halfway up a steep rise, the team laboring in the traces. Perpendicular walls of smooth mica on both sides of the trail kept the passengers from getting a clear aim from inside.

"Gee up!" the frightened driver called out, lashing his team to a frenzy. "Haw, gee up!"

More gunfire sounded from above, and Jeanette heard the slugs thwacking into the japanned wood of the coach. She heard the sharp, precision crack of Maddox's carbine, once, twice; then abruptly his weapon fell silent and a body slumped past the window. Jeanette watched, horrified, as the seriously wounded young sharpshooter lost his hold on the box and fell directly in the path of the right front wheel. It snapped his spine like a dry twig, the coach momentarily jolting as it rolled over him.

Another flurry of slugs, and she heard the driver cry out. Major Carmichael, his soft face as pale as alkali dust, made no move to draw his Army .44. Legget had his pin-fire revolver in his hand but could spot no target.

"We're being attacked!" Carmichael repeated uselessly, almost blubbering. "Cheyennes! We're being attacked! Maddox is dead, we're being attacked—"

"Shut up, you fat, white-livered coward and draw steel!" Legget growled. "Ma'am, you get the hell down!"

His warning came too late. The next flurry of slugs ripped into the leather seats, and Jeanette felt a white-hot crease of pain in her left side.

"She's been hit!" Legget shouted to Carmichael even as Jeanette almost fainted. "Tend to her!"

But the blubbering major ignored her. "Maddox is dead!" he said. "Oh, sweet Jesus, Maddox is dead, Cheyennes killed him!"

"You talk too damn much," Woodrow Denton said.

The man he spoke to was called Lumpy because of a huge goiter distending the side of his neck.

"The hell you mean, Woody? I swear by the twin balls o' Napoleon I ain't opened my mouth onc't since we vamoosed with the swag!"

"I mean during the holdup, you fool. You're

spozed to be an Indian. Indians don't talk so damn much."

Denton, Lumpy, and four other men nearly filled the single room of a run-down ,shack. It was hidden high on a remote ridge well behind Fort Randall. One of the men was a cavalry captain in full field uniform. The rest were all dressed as Northern Cheyenne braves. Their authentic masquerade included horse-hair "braids" and skin darkened by berry juice.

"What the hell," Lumpy told his leader. "Don't I toss in plenty of Cheyenne words? Anyway, it was your big idea, seein' as how I can palaver a little Cheyenne, that I should do the talking."

"You're spozed to sound like a Cheyenne that speaks a little English. That means plenty of grunts and baby talk. Hell, soon as you opened your mouth that woman stared at you like she twigged the whole game."

"She didn't twig a damn thing. She had other problems," Lumpy said. "Hell, she was bleedin' like a stuck pig."

When he heard this, the cavalry officer's jaw slacked open in astonished disbelief. He had been perched on the edge of a deal table, portioning out piles of gold dust while the others spoke. Now he slowly laid down a chamois pouch he was filling and rose from the table. He was big and powerfully built, with blunt features and a permanent sneer of cold command.

"You *shot* Jeanette Lofley?" Captain Seth Carlson demanded. "It wasn't enough you killed the guard and a passenger? One of you idiotic, horseshit-for-brains morons also *shot* the Old Man's wife?"

"Don't get all your pennies in a bunch," Denton said. "It was a accident, is all. We had to spray 'em good with lead before the driver and all the passengers would throw down their irons. She just got in front of a stray round, is all."

"Is *all?* You fools! *I'm* the one in charge of the new mountain company. These Indians are my direct responsibility. Why do you think I know about all the shipments? You know damn well the treaty outlaws military patrols along the wagon road, but not elsewhere. Until now the Old Man's been more or less content with my progress in hunting down Shoots Left Handed's band. Now that you've shot his wife, he's going to want Cheyenne guts for garters. Did you kill her?"

Denton shrugged, looking ridiculous now that he had removed his bonnet and fake braids. The berry dye stopped where his bald white head took over.

"Hard to tell. I couldn't see if she was gut-shot or caught one in the cage."

Everyone there knew what he meant. A gut shot would bleed internally. This far from civilization, such wounds were often fatal. A shot to the rib cage bled less and was usually easier to survive.

"If she dies," Carlson said, "you can put this down in your book—our little gold mine has just run dry. Lofley knows he doesn't stand a chance of making the general's list, so he's not exactly champing at the bit to fight savages. But he dotes on his wife. Even if she doesn't die, he won't rest until every Cheyenne in this region has been hunted down. That means more pressure on me."

"What I don't get," Denton said, "is why it's so all-fired important to you to pin this on Cheyennes? Most of them are concentrated down around the Powder and the Rosebud. It'd be more sensible-like to hang it on Blackfeet or Mandans. Then you could just kill off a few 'n' show their scalps to your boss, tell him you got the renegades."

Carlson frowned impatiently. "Think about it. There's thousands of Blackfeet in this area, fewer than two hundred Cheyennes. What happens if you're a Blackfoot warrior and you hear somebody is dressing up like your tribe to rob whites? You go on the warpath. This Cheyenne band is too weak."

All this was true. But neither Denton nor any of the hardcases riding for him knew the secret history of Carlson's one-man war against the Cheyenne nation. Indeed, they knew nothing of the humiliating debacle which had sent him to this godforsaken outpost.

It had begun years earlier, at Fort Bates in the Wyoming Territory. While still a shavetail lieutenant, he had fallen in love with Kristen, daughter of the wealthy mustang rancher Hiram Steele. Then he had discovered, about the same time Hiram did, that Kristen was meeting secretly with Matthew Hanchon—a full-blooded Cheyenne in spite of his white name.

Enraged, Hiram Steele ordered one of his wranglers to savagely beat Hanchon. And Hanchon was warned he would be killed if he ever met with the girl again. But Carlson took no chances. He looked the youth up on his own and warned him: Either Matthew left the territory for good, or his white parents' lucrative contract with Fort Bates went to another mercantile.

The plan worked. Then everything went to hell in a hay wagon. Hiram Steele went on to drive the Hanchons out of their mercantile business. When they sold out and started a mustang spread, Steele decided to run them off with Carlson's help. What they hadn't counted on was Matthew Hanchon's return as a Cheyenne warrior.

Even now, just thinking about what had happened made Carlson's face flush warm with shame and anger. Hanchon had humiliated him at every turn! While attacking the buck on the open plains, the officer's horse had stepped into a prairie-dog hole and thrown Carlson ass-over-applecart in front of all his men. Then the buck and his renegade companion had whipped Carlson and three men from the dragoons, thwarting the effort to drive the Hanchons from their spread. Worse yet, a subsequent investigation had turned up Carlson's falsified reconnaissance reports designed to create an "Indian menace." As punishment, he'd been sent to this northern hellhole where, in winter, piss froze before it hit the ground.

Denton had watched Carlson's face closely. Now he shook his head and said, "Whatever you say, trooper. 'Pears to me, though, you're nursin' a grudge agin the Cheyenne."

"Well, iffen he is," Lumpy said, fingering his goiter and eagerly watching Carlson fill another pouch with gold dust, "he's got a perfect job for grinding axes."

Carlson commanded a new mountain company which represented the U.S. Army's latest Indian-fighting strategy. Hitherto the Army had tried to engage the savages in combat on the plains. But this had proved suicidal. By warm weather the new grass left Indian ponies strong and agile, and they could cover up to seventy miles a day relying on water holes known only to them. Once they fled into the mountains, there was no finding them. The Army's response was to equip smaller, lighter, faster units for high-altitude fighting and hunt the Indians down, concentrating massive firepower on them and exterminating them without allowing surrender or taking prisoners.

"Maybe he has," Denton said, "but so far ol' Shoots Left Handed has slipped through his fingers slicker 'n grease through a goose, ain't that the straight?"

Denton's mocking tone irritated Carlson. The man looked like a sinister clown, his face painted dark beneath the fish-belly white of his pate. He was scum, and Carlson would gladly air him in a minute if he weren't so useful. And one glance around at his filthy companions, all hardcases on the prod, reminded him that only Denton could control these animals.

"So far he has," Carlson admitted. "But time is a bird, my friend, and the bird is on the wing."

Chapter Three

For three full sleeps Touch the Sky and Little Horse rode hard, bearing north toward the Always Star and the Land of the Grandmother.

The sacred Black Hills constantly behind their left shoulder, they forded the Little Bighorn, the Bighorn, and the Yellowstone. Following Arrow Keeper's urgent instructions, they pushed their mounts to the limits of endurance. Cottonwood groves and open, rolling plains slowly gave way to towering evergreen forests and deep coulees still moist with snow runoff. Fortunately, water and lush grass were plentiful. On the third day, the Bear Paw Mountains loomed up on the distant horizon.

Little Horse had been absorbed in deep thought for some time.

"Brother," he said when they paused to water their ponies at the Milk River, "I know Shoots

Left Handed and most in his band. You saw them at the annual Sun Dance, again at the Chief Renewal. They are a generous and peaceful group and always bring many blankets and horses for the poor during the dances."

"I remember them well. They were the only Cheyenne band still wearing fur leggings in spring."

"At one time they lived closer to our Powder River hunting grounds. But Shoots Left Handed married an Assiniboin and fell in love with the north country. His wife died, but he stayed in the north. Soon other members of his Cheyenne clan migrated to join him. Now he is a peace leader of his own band.

"He fought beside Arrow Keeper at Wolf Creek and saved his life from a Kiowa throwing ax. So I am not surprised that Arrow Keeper is quick to send us during this trouble. But that is not the only reason he wanted us—*you*—out of camp immediately. And why was our leaving a secret, unless he does not want your enemies within the tribe to follow you?"

Touch the Sky listened carefully to all this, saying nothing. While he listened he gazed off at the distant mountains. From here they did indeed resemble bear paws, huge and blunt with snowcapped toes. Looking at them made him recall the time a grizzly had trapped him in a cave at Medicine Lake.

"Yes," he finally replied, "Arrow Keeper knows the danger well. When he sent me by myself to Medicine Lake, Wolf Who Hunts Smiling and

Swift Canoe followed and tried to send me under. This time Arrow Keeper wants to make sure the dogs do not return to their vomit."

By now their ponies had nearly drunk their fill. To avoid suspicion as long as possible, Arrow Keeper had instructed them to leave their own ponies with the herd. Instead, he had them cut out two from his own string. Little Horse rode a ginger buckskin, Touch the Sky a blood bay with a pure white blaze on its forehead. Like all ponies owned by Arrow Keeper, these had been taught special tricks and blessed with strong medicine.

"You are worried about Honey Eater," Little Horse said, not making it a question.

Touch the Sky nodded. His lips were set in a grim, determined slit. "I am worried, buck. Your words fly straight-arrow. Black Elk is sick with jealous hatred. At least in camp my presence served as a constant reminder that he must pay dearly for hurting her. Now I am gone, and who knows for how long?"

"Is this why you took Two Twists aside before we rode out?"

Again Touch the Sky nodded. Two Twists was a junior warrior in training. He had fought gallantly alongside Touch the Sky and Little Horse in freeing Cheyenne prisoners from the Comanche stronghold in Blanco Canyon. Touch the Sky had instructed him to keep a close eye on Honey Eater, especially when Black Elk was around. Touch the Sky had already served notice to Black Elk. Unlike the barbaric Comanche, Cheyenne law did not permit wife-slaughter and wife-beating. If he laid a hand on Honey Eater one more time, he was carrion fodder.

Touch the Sky's bay snorted and backed away from the water, having drunk its fill. Now, as they prepared to ride on, both youths again gazed toward the Bear Paws.

Again they were riding into the maw of unknown danger. Not only was this area crawling with Blackfeet and other hostile tribes, but with blue-bloused soldiers too. And with Cheyenne being blamed for the recent attacks Arrow Keeper spoke of, they were open targets for vigilante fire.

Therefore they had come well-armed. Touch the Sky's percussion-action Sharps protruded from his scabbard, Little Horse's four-shot, revolving-barrel shotgun from his. Both braves were also armed with knives, stone-headed throwing axes, and new green bows. Their foxskin quivers were crammed with fire-hardened arrows.

"It is time to ride, brother," Touch the Sky said, gripping his pony's hackamore.

The tall, broad-shouldered youth cast one last, long glance south toward their Powder River camp. His eyes were clouded with trouble as he thought about Honey Eater. Then, pointing their hair bridles toward the Bear Paws, they rode on into the gathering twilight and unknown trouble.

Almost three sleeps had passed before Wolf Who Hunts Smiling was sure of it. He turned to Swift Canoe and suddenly said, "Brother, we have less brains between us than a rabbit. Woman Face and Little Horse are gone!"

Swift Canoe glanced up, startled. The two youths sat before Wolf Who Hunts Smiling's tipi. Their sister the sun had gone to her rest earlier. Now the two braves were filing arrow points in the light of a bright cottonwood fire.

"Gone? What do you mean?"

"Buck, do I suddenly speak Arapaho? What else does 'gone' mean? I mean gone, they are not in camp! Have you seen them?"

Swift Canoe thought about it hard, the furrow between his eyes deepening. Then he shook his head. "You are right, Panther Clan."

They had been sent out secretly by Arrow Keeper. Wolf Who Hunts Smiling knew that. Once before, the wily old shaman had sent Woman Face away to avoid danger in camp. Only this time, he had not announced his decision at council. And the two friends had taken different ponies.

"It would be foolish," Wolf Who Hunts Smiling said, "to trail them now. The sign will be cold. And Arrow Keeper would miss us and know."

"This time," Swift Canoe said, disappointed, "they have played the fox and outwitted us."

"Perhaps not, Cheyenne. Only think on this thing. Did Arrow Keeper announce the departure from camp of Little Horse and Woman Face, as is custom and law?"

Swift Canoe shook his head, confused. "You know he did not. You just said—"

"And the others in camp? Soon now these two

37

must be missed. When they are, the people will be furious to know. After all, these two have never cleared their names from serious charges that they have spied for Long Knives. But what if, before Arrow Keeper can concoct a story, *another* story flies through camp on the wind?"

"What story, brother?"

"Put those points down and follow me, buck. I know my cousin will want to counsel with us on this matter."

The two youths stayed in the apron of shadows at the edge of the main clearing. Slipping behind tipis and lodges, they avoided the groups where soldier societies had gathered to smoke and talk. Soon they stood before Black Elk's tipi. A bright fire burned within, and they could see two long, distorted shadows: Black Elk and Honey Eater.

Black Elk's voice raged from within.

"You will *not* take this tone with me and make me a squaw, haughty Cheyenne she-bitch! I am your husband and this tribe's war leader. I have cut off your braid before, and what man has done, man can do."

"Brother," Swift Canoe said nervously, "Black Elk has blood in his eyes. This is not a wise time to interrupt."

"You are wrong, brother," Wolf Who Hunts Smiling said, his furtive grin dividing his face. Anger seethed inside him. His coup feathers had been the soul of his medicine bag, and thanks to Woman Face they were now a memory smell, a thing of smoke.

"No better time," he added. "This hatred in my

cousin's voice, who do you think has caused it? None other than Woman Face!"

Wolf Who Hunts Smiling stepped boldly forward and stood before the entrance flap.

"Black Elk! I would speak with you."

The flap was thrust wide and Black Elk stared out at the visitors, scowling. The fire inside backlighted his face and braided hair. The wrinkled, leathery flap of sewn-on ear made him look fierce in the eerie orange light.

"Well?" he demanded. "Are you a totem pole, or is there a bone caught in your throat? Speak!"

But the younger brave had hesitated because Honey Eater stood close to the entrance. Even Wolf Who Hunts Smiling, whose great ambition for leadership left him indifferent to women, was suddenly impressed yet again with her frail beauty. High, delicately sculpted cheekbones framed an oval face and full lips. Her hair had finally grown back long enough to braid with her usual white columbine petals. Her huge, wing-shaped eyes watched the three braves suspiciously, knowing some new treachery was afoot.

Wolf Who Hunts Smiling signaled to his cousin with his eyes, then looked at Honey Eater again.

"Back off, mooncalf!" Black Elk snapped at her.

When she was gone, Wolf Who Hunts Smiling said, "Black Elk, have you seen Woman Face or Little Horse these past several sleeps?"

Slowly, Black Elk's frown turned into a look of wary curiosity. His cousin was not one to make small talk.

"Woman Face I rarely see anymore," he said. "He wisely avoids me and my clan circle. But now I recall that Little Horse should be riding herd guard, yet I have not seen him. Do not be coy. We are not girls in their sewing lodge. Why do you ask this thing?"

"Cousin, two of Arrow Keeper's best ponies are missing. So are Woman Face and Little Horse. Yet nothing was said at council. Do you see? The old shaman has sent them on a secret mission in violation of tribal law. Even Chief Gray Thunder cannot authorize missions without a vote of the Headmen. Only the Star Chamber can do this, and they have not convened."

For many heartbeats Black Elk was silent, thinking about this.

"Cousin," Wolf Who Hunts Smiling continued, speaking faster in his gathering excitement, "you know there is bad feeling within the tribe for these two. This, ever since they deserted their people to fight for Woman Face's white family. Now, any time they ride out, the people talk. They say, 'This Touch the Sky, why does he ride off so much without the camp crier announcing it? Why so much secret business for this one?' "

Black Elk was catching on. A faint smile touched his stern lips. There was grudging admiration in his tone when he said, "I have ears for this, cousin. As you say, nothing was told at council."

"Nothing. And cousin, do you recall? River of Winds recently scouted the Valley of the Greasy

Grass for buffalo sign. He spotted blue-bloused soldiers camped there."

Black Elk nodded, suddenly very impressed by his younger cousin's scheming mind. He said, "No one would believe either of us. It is commonly known we would gladly feed his liver to the dogs. But cousin, you and I have brothers in our Bull Whip soldier troop. They will gladly claim to have seen Woman Face and Little Horse playing the white man's Indian for soldiers."

Touch the Sky and Little Horse rode as far into the mountains as they could before night settled over everything like a dark cloak. They made a cold camp beside a runoff stream. A meager meal consisted of cold water, and pemmican and dried plums from their legging sashes.

The next morning, as the word-bringer Goes Ahead had promised, they found signs where Shoots Left Handed's band had blazed a trail to their latest camp. For the better part of a day the two youths climbed steadily higher and higher. The trees held as they rose, but grew thinner and more wind-twisted. Deadfalls, piles of rock scree, mud slides caused by spring runoff blocked the way. But all this also, the two young braves realized, made it tougher for enemies to find this camp.

Finally, climbing up out of a long cutbank, they were greeted by the owl hoot of a friendly Cheyenne sentry. He led the new arrivals to the high-altitude camp which had been made in the lee of a well-protected ridge.

The squalor of the place shocked and saddened both youths. Dogs were always numerous in Cheyenne camps because of their usefulness as sentries, but they had all long since been eaten. The few ponies which remained were starvation-thin, their ribs protruding like barrel staves. It was foaling time for the mares, but they were too weak to birth. The pony-loving Cheyennes would cry openly as they were forced to kill the mares and cut the new foals out.

Nonetheless, life went on. Water haulers made the long trip from the nearest stream, full bladder-bags sloshing. Old women sat in a circle pre-paring precious chokecherries, gathered earlier after hours of hard scouring. There was no other food.

"Tonight," Shoots Left Handed said, soon after meeting the new arrivals, "we will eat another pony."

His words shocked them into silence. Tribal history told of times, of course, when Cheyennes had been forced to kill and eat ponies. And they knew that such tribes as the Apache ate horse meat as casually as they might eat buffalo or elk. But never had they seen Cheyennes forced to such barbarism.

They sat in a small circle in Shoots Left Handed's tipi, a fire blazing in the pit to counter the cold mountain air. The group included Pawnee Killer, the band's battle leader.

"Our band has lost many warriors because of these attacks against whites," Pawnee Killer said.

He was a brave with perhaps 40 winters behind

him, still vigorous and strong though his braids were traced with silver. He wore a leather shirt adorned with the intricate Cheyenne beadwork admired throughout the West.

"Warriors are not the end of it," Shoots Left Handed said. The old peace chief had left his snow-white hair unbraided, and a milky cataract clouded one eye. Hunger had emaciated the entire tribe, and their leader had not been spared. Touch the Sky winced when he noticed that the fingers clutching the old man's blanket about him were as thin as twigs.

"These constant attacks by pony soldiers," he continued, "have forced us further and further into these barren mountains. This is intolerable. We are Cheyenne, plains-loving horsemen! My people are sick, miserable, hungry, and tired of eating fish."

"Too," Pawnee Killer said, "all this constant moving to new camps puts us at risk from attack by the Piegan."

Touch the Sky and Little Horse nodded, recognizing the name by which the Blackfoot tribe called itself.

Touch the Sky said, "Would the Piegan disguise themselves as Cheyenne and attack whites?"

"As a people," Pawnee Killer said, "they are as low as the lice-eating Pawnee. Yes, they are capable of such a thing. But for many winters now they have stayed well south of the Milk River Road. Nor are they a tribe to bother with such games as dressing up."

"Truly," Touch the Sky said, nodding, "I know

of no red tribe that plays at such games, though our Lakota cousins will dress in a blue blouse after they kill a soldier."

Pawnee Killer watched the tall newcomer closely, his eyes slitted in an approving scrutiny. "As you say, young Cheyenne. I see that your mind flies on the same wind with mine. This painting and dressing for crime is more of a white man's game."

Outside the tipi, the cold mountain wind whipped up to a blustering frenzy, driving everyone for shelter. Touch the Sky heard a starving horse nicker piteously, heard a sick baby crying with a steady, faint tone of utter hopelessness. Hot tears threatened his eyes as he realized: All around him, the people who shared his blood were dying.

"We must find out at once who is making these attacks," he declared with conviction. "And the tribe must be blessed with strong medicine. When were the Arrows last renewed?"

Pawnee Killer shook his head, making the cut-off sign as he mentioned the dead. "Scalp Cane was our Arrow Keeper. But he lay sick for several moons before he crossed over, unable to renew the Arrows."

Alarm tightened the young shaman apprentice's face. "Are they safe?"

"Of course. They are with White Plume of the Sky Walker Clan. But he is not a shaman. We have no priest to conduct the ceremony."

"I will conduct the renewal soon," Touch the Sky said. "Not just for the warriors, but to cleanse the entire tribe."

Chief Shoots Left Handed nodded. His milky eye glistened in the flickering firelight.

"This is a good thing, little brother. I knew Arrow Keeper would send the right brave. But I fear strong medicine alone cannot spare us from the new Bluecoat mountain troop. Even now their turncoat Ute scouts are sniffing out this camp, and soon the attack will again be on us."

Chapter Four

Colonel Orrin Lofley said, "You know my motto, Carlson: The shit rolls downhill."

"Yes, sir," Captain Seth Carlson replied, thinking to himself as usual: *Why don't you set it to music, you tiresome blowhard?* But the silver eagles perched on Lofley's epaulets stared at the captain with stern, unblinking authority.

"That was my *wife* who got shot in this last attack, Carlson!"

"Yes, sir. The colonel has my deepest regrets. Is Mrs. Lofley doing better?"

"She's going to survive, Carlson, no thanks to you. Your deepest regrets aren't worth a plug nickel. You're in charge of what's supposed to be the best Indian-hunting company in the Far West. I don't want regrets from you, I want action."

"Yes, sir."

The commanding officer of remote Fort Randall was a short, barrel-chested redhead with coarse-grained skin and a weak chin disguised by a goatee. His left arm had been partially paralyzed during the Sioux campaigns. He could not lift it above his shoulder and required assistance in taking his jacket off. But if a man could walk and still had one functioning trigger finger, Army regulations permitted him to serve.

"Carlson, this fort is already the butt of jokes back East. Every shitbird recruit who can't open his mess kit gets posted here. I'm sick of cringing every time the newspapers arrive, crammed full of stories about how the goddamn aboriginal hostiles are making a mockery of the U.S. Army! Now that my own wife has eaten an Indian bullet, you think the papers aren't rawhiding me mercilessly?"

"Yes, sir. I mean, no, sir."

Carlson knew damn well that Lofley only had himself to blame for his troubles. He had ended up at Fort Randall because his inept battlefield tactics were infamous in military circles. In one campaign against the Hunkpapa Sioux, a regiment directly under his command had expended 25,000 rounds of ammunition in killing five Sioux, all women and children. Carlson's unit of mountain-trained sharpshooters, in contrast, had once wiped out an entire Assiniboin camp and expended only 500 rounds. The trick, Carlson knew, was to hit them in their sleep and shoot plumb for their vitals.

"The Army is caught between the sap and the

bark on this Indian question," Lofley said, standing up from his desk. Behind him on the wall was a Mercator map of the United States. The all-important 100th meridian was marked with a heavy black line. This was the crucial boundary where rainfall dramatically slacked off and the tall grasses gave way to the shortgrass prairie— marking the official beginning of Plains Indian country.

"If the damned Indian lovers back East hadn't tied my hands in Congress, I would by God put paid to it *now*, Carlson, and make this region safe for white women like Jeanette to travel."

"Yes, sir."

"But even if that damned Laramie Accord forbids a major command offensive, it permits punitive actions away from the wagon road right of way. That's where your new company comes in, Carlson. Damn it, Soldier Blue, find those heathen Cheyennes and kill every man, woman, and child! That's an order!"

"Yes, sir. We've been trying."

"My grandmother *tries*, Carlson. You don't seem to understand me here. It's not just the fact that those mother-rutting savages almost killed my wife. The War Department is giving me six sorts of hell, not to mention the local vigilantes who cry about how soft the Army is on Indians. So help me Hannah, I want those red devils exterminated. Your unit's been crackerjack when it comes to routing out Mandans and such. Why so much trouble with one raggedy-assed band of Cheyennes?"

Carlson felt the irony of his situation. The plan to blame stagecoach and freight-wagon attacks on Cheyennes had served two very useful purposes: It made him rich, and it built a strong case to justify his eventual slaughter of Shoots Left Handed and his band, thus appeasing Carlson's vendetta against Matthew Hanchon and the Cheyenne nation.

So in the beginning, he had deliberately not tried to wipe out the band quickly. Their continued existence guaranteed scapegoats for the attacks by Woodrow Denton and his gun-throwers. But when the pressure to punish the Cheyennes had finally mounted, the band had slipped off to more remote regions. Now they had to be tracked down. But scouts were on the trail and due to report any day now.

Lofley turned to the map and jabbed at it with an angry index finger.

"*Look* at this region, Carlson. We're responsible for thousands of square miles of mountains and forests and canyons so deep you can't see the bottoms on a clear day. I have one special mountain company—yours—outfitted for the field. The rest are regular cavalry.

"Does anyone care that the goddamn manual says twenty-five miles a day is the maximum for the regular cavalry? I said twenty-five miles a day. And we're locking horns with Indians who ride with as many as five remounts on their string, remounts as clever and well-trained as circus ponies. They carry nothing but their weapons, they live on bark and insects if they

49

have to, and they ride up to eighty miles a day."

Carlson mechanically said his "yes, sir" again, his eyes glazing over. Lofley was a bitter man with an ax to grind. He had repeated all of this so often he sounded like a salivating bible-thumper.

Finally he dismissed his subordinate. But as Carlson was about to escape through the office door, Lofley called his name.

"Sir?"

"You know the Officer Promotion Board meets next month at Fort Union?"

"Yes, sir."

"You have enough time in grade. If I sign the recommendation, the promotion to major is almost guaranteed."

Carlson nodded, liking what he was hearing.

"I also know how bad you want to get transferred back East. Just remember, appointment to major makes you a field-grade officer. That means you post out to a new command. I can't guarantee the East. But if you were to exterminate these Cheyennes, that would give you a Letter of Merit in your file, maybe even a Letter of Commendation. That would strengthen your request considerably."

Carlson nodded again, liking it even better. The scheme with the attacks was about played out anyway. If he could not only kill his enemies, the Cheyenne, but also earn a promotion and a transfer, so much the better.

"They shot my wife," Lofley repeated before he dismissed him. "Carlson, kill those damn hostiles. And bring me their scalps to show the paper-collar newspaper boys!"

"Goes Ahead should have returned by now," the battle chief named Pawnee Killer said.

He, Touch the Sky, and Little Horse were crossing toward the tipi of White Plume. The tribe elders had agreed with Touch the Sky that a Renewal of the Arrows should be held immediately; any strategy to combat Bluecoats or the highway raiders was doomed to fail without good magic.

Goes Ahead had been sent south to Powder River with news of this disaster. He was to have returned immediately, circling by way of Fort Randall to scout the soldier's activity.

"If enemies have slain him," Pawnee Killer added, "our tribe has lost a warrior who fights like ten men."

It was mid-morning of Touch the Sky's first full day in the high-altitude camp. Nights in the Bear Paws were cold, and he had shivered even in the depths of his shaggy buffalo robe. The cries of the hungry children were piteous. In the morning he and Little Horse had refused their portion of cooked meat, knowing it was horse flesh. They'd subsisted on the last of the pemmican and dried fruit in their sashes.

Now, as they picked their way across the sloping, rock-strewn ground, Touch the Sky glanced warily all around them. The camp seemed safely located, at first glance. They were deep in the lee of a sheltered ridge, cut off from sunshine but also from sight below. Three approaches were blocked by cliffs, landslides, and steep escarpments of rock. Night and day vigilant sentries watched the only path leading into camp.

All seemed secure enough. Yet during the night Touch the Sky had followed Arrow Keeper's advice: He had closed his mind to all thought and simply listened to the language of his senses. And then abruptly, like being plunged naked into a snowbank, his entire body had felt a bone-numbing chill of premonition.

Some danger lurked near this camp. He was sure of it. Lurked very near. And Little Horse, who had long ago recognized his friend's big medicine and the mulberry birthmark buried in his hair as the mark of the warrior—he too saw this knowledge in Touch the Sky's troubled dark eyes.

Something else had plagued him during the cold, windy night—a gnawing in his belly as sharp as a rat's incisors. For how could he forget that Honey Eater was living with a man who was on the feather edge of killing her? Leaving her with Black Elk was like deserting her in a grizzly's den.

But he forced his thoughts back to the here and now when the group of braves reached White Plume's tipi. White Plume, a brave with perhaps 50 winters behind him, looked at the two visitors with genuine respect when he learned Arrow Keeper had sent them. He ushered them into his tipi. His wife filled a clay pipe for them. Then she discreetly ducked outside to visit her clan while the men counseled over their important business.

"You are a shaman?" White Plume asked Touch the Sky after all had smoked to the directions.

He shook his head. "I assist Arrow Keeper at the ceremonies, and he is teaching me the shaman arts."

White Plume was satisfied with this response. "I know Arrow Keeper, buck. When I was a limber sapling even younger than you, he was once my battle chief in a fight against Crows. With so many arrows in him he looked like a porcupine, he rallied thirty Cheyennes to victory against twice as many stub-hands. If he chose you to assist him, this means you surely have the gift of visions and are blessed with strong medicine. He would not have chosen you otherwise."

He did not press the issue. It was understood among Indians that spiritual matters were powerful and mostly private. A person who possessed the gift of visions was not expected to speak of this thing, nor were others welcome to mention it.

White Plume crossed to the rear of his tipi and lifted aside a flat buffalo-hide saddle he'd won in a pony race with a Dakota. He pulled aside a blanket, then returned with a soft coyote-fur pouch.

All four men fell silent as he unwrapped the Medicine Arrows in the flickering firelight. There were four of them, painted in bright blue and yellow stripes and fletched with scarlet feathers. Ten sets in all existed, one for each of the ten bands of the Shaiyena nation.

Arrow Keeper had explained carefully how the secret of the Arrows had first been revealed to the people by the High Holy Ones who lived in the northern lights, The Land Where the Food Comes From. The fate of the Arrows was the fate of the entire tribe. Therefore, it was the Arrow Keeper's solemn responsibility to not only protect them with his life, but to keep them forever sweet and clean. Certain serious crimes—such as murder and adultery—stained the Arrows and thus the tribe. The Renewal of the Arrows was held to cleanse them after a crime or to strengthen them before a battle.

In the presence of the Arrows, Touch the Sky unconsciously lowered his voice. "Tell your warriors," he said to Pawnee Killer, "to paint and dress and bring their gifts to the Arrows. But tell the rest too to bring gifts. The entire tribe must renew its medicine and dance."

Pawnee Killer nodded, but his voice was heavy with doubt. "I will certainly tell my warriors, Touch the Sky. What few remain to us. Arrow Keeper is right, our strong medicine must be renewed. But medicine or no, this new Bluecoat mountain troop, they are wild and crazy like dogs in the hot moons. If our camp is located one more time, there will be one less band of Cheyenne."

The Cheyenne brave died hard.

Rough Feather, a huge Ute scout employed by Fort Randall, had nearly been taken by surprise. For many sleeps now, Rough Feather had painstakingly hunted down this camp. The Utes were a mountain tribe, nimble as goats and highly useful to the U.S. Army. After numerous false starts and miles of useless back-tracking, he had finally gained sight of Shoots Left Handed's camp.

Eluding the sentries in the gathering twilight had been tricky and required long patience. Finally, after crawling on his belly for hours over rocks, he knew right where the heart of camp was. He made a mental picture of everything so Carlson could plan a precise strike: the layout of the tipis, the number and location of sentries, any possible escape routes.

That Captain Carlson, thought Rough Feather—*here* was no white devil to fool with. The motto of his Indian-fighting company was known to every tribe in the region: *Take no prisoners!* The Utes had seen this coming early on, and wisely decided to nail their streamers to the Bluecoat mast.

Thinking all of these things, intent on looking ahead at the camp, he had almost missed the approach of a rider behind him.

The young Cheyenne did not spot him until he was almost on him. His pony suddenly snorted and pulled up short, tossing its head violently. In a heartbeat the Cheyenne's streamered lance was raised for the throw.

Rough Feather was faster. There was already a jagged rock in his hand. The big Ute rose to his feet and sent it flying hard. It chunked into the Cheyenne's forehead with an ominous sound of bone splitting. He slid from his pony like a heavy sack of grain. Moments later the young buck's moccasined heels futilely scratched the dirt as Rough Feather's French dagger opened his throat from ear to ear.

Rough Feather cursed this bad luck. He wiped his blade in the grass, then quickly hobbled the pony to keep it from wandering on into camp. But hiding the body, this close to camp and with such barren ground cover, was not worth the risk. Now he would have to leave immediately.

But soon Rough Feather calmed down. After all, even though the raggedy band would be alerted, what could they do? They were at the end of their tether. Moving an entire camp was a major enterprise. So many sick elders and infants made it far harder. Now they were trapped between the last mountain strongholds and the approaching Bluecoats.

Even as Rough Feather began to ease back down the trail, the night wind rose to a shriek like the howl of wolves mating.

Chapter Five

That night, while young women kept time with stone-filled gourds, everyone in Shoots Left Handed's band danced at the Renewal of the Arrows ceremony.

Touch the Sky directed that even the outlying sentries should be relieved long enough to join the dance. He had feared, at first, that the people would be too weak from hunger to dance. But hunger did not matter once the rhythmic cadence of stones and the steady *"Hi-ya, hii-ya"* chant started sounding. Everyone old enough to dance was soon circling a well-hidden ceremonial fire.

Touch the Sky watched them, his clay-painted face gruesome, yet magnificent, in the wavering glow of the fire. Their knees kicked high, higher, the starvation-lean bodies wrapped in furs against the mountain chill. And as they danced their

57

misery out of them, hunger made the trance-state happen faster.

For a moment, watching them, Touch the Sky felt the power of his epic vision at Medicine Lake. Again the images were laid over his eyes: He saw red men, thousands of them from every tribe west of the river called Great Waters, all dancing as one people, dancing out their misery and fear and utter hopelessness. And on the horizon behind them, guidons snapping in the wind, sabers gleaming in the blood-red sun, the approaching hordes of blue-bloused soldiers.

When all seems lost, the voice of the dead Chief Yellow Bear had warned him, *become your enemy.* Touch the Sky felt the bitter sting of the present irony. Clearly, an enemy of the Cheyenne had become *them.*

After the dance, Touch the Sky unwrapped the Medicine Arrows and laid them on a stump in the center of camp. He had donned his mountain-lion skin, a gift from Arrow Keeper. It had been blessed with strong medicine, the shaman insisted. Touch the Sky could not swear to this. But he had worn it during a vicious Comanche raid, drawing all their fire onto himself, and not one bullet or arrow had found his flesh.

For this ceremony, he had painted his face as Cheyenne braves paint for war: forehead yellow, nose red, chin black. He also wore his single-horned war bonnet, its tail long with coup feathers. As the tribe lined up to leave their gifts

to the Arrows, the crying of hungry babes rose
to join the keening wail of the night wind. The
misery of this people was evident in their lean
bodies and empty stares.

For this reason, Touch the Sky recited the
sacred Renewal Prayer in his clearest, most
powerful voice, a voice meant to inspire the
people with hope:

> *Oh, Great Spirit of Maiyun,*
> *whose voice we hear in the winds,*
> *and whose breath gives life to all the world,*
> *hear us! We are small and weak, we need*
> *your strength and wisdom.*

"Let this be so," the people said as one.

> *Let us walk in beauty, and make our eyes*
> *ever behold the red and purple sunset.*
> *Make our hearts respect the things you have*
> *made and our ears sharp to hear your voice.*
> *Make us wise that we may understand the*
> *things you have taught the people.*

"Let this be so," the others repeated.

> *Let us learn the lessons you have hidden*
> *in every leaf and rock.*
> *We seek strength, not to be greater than our*
> *brothers, but to fight our greatest enemy*
> *—ourselves.*
> *Make us always ready to come to you with*
> *clean hands and straight eyes.*

"Let this be so," the tribe sang as one.

Now Touch the Sky's voice rose above the shrieking of the wind, concluding the Renewal Prayer in a powerful tone that echoed downridge.

So when life fades, as the fading sunset,
our spirits may come to you
without shame.

A long, profound silence followed the prayer. Then Touch the Sky's voice again rang out: "Cheyenne people! The Arrows have been renewed! Now leave your gifts!"

One by one, every member of the tribe with more than 12 winters behind him knelt beside the Arrows to leave a sacrifice. The tribe's desperate situation was mirrored in the value of the gifts. Though everyone left something, there were no valuable pelts, no rich tobacco, few weapons. Instead, there were brightly dyed feathers, decorated coup sticks, moccasins with beaded soles.

The last gift had just been placed near the stump when there was a frightened shout from the direction of the only entrance to camp.

Everyone stared toward the narrow path. One of the sentries, who had been relieved and was riding into camp to leave his gift, frantically beckoned to them. As one, the tribe hurried across to him.

Darkness had descended, but a full moon owned the unclouded sky. The dead brave, Goes Ahead, was clear in the luminous white moonlight. He lay sprawled on his back, arms far-flung, his neck opened up like a second mouth. His pony was hobbled nearby. The huge gash in Goes Ahead's forehead told how he had been dropped from his pony.

Raven's Wing, the dead brave's young bride, cried out. She dropped beside her man and blindly groped for a sharp piece of flint in the rough dirt. No one stopped her when she began savagely gouging her arms with it, drawing ribbons of blood. But several of her clan sisters automatically formed a ring around her, blocking access to more serious weapons.

A few other Cheyennes made the cut-off sign while an old grandmother began keening in grief for the fallen youth.

Touch the Sky and Little Horse locked glances in the moonlight. The awful significance of this death, so near camp and the time of the sacred Renewal, could not be denied.

Shoots Left Handed and Pawnee Killer were clearly thinking the same thing. They crossed to join the young Cheyennes.

"The Arrows have been renewed," Shoots Left Handed said. "Good. It was a good ceremony, a good prayer. But clearly, Goes Ahead did not fall on his knife. He was murdered. That means our camp has been discovered yet again. Our enemy knows where we are—soon comes the attack!"

Touch the Sky and Little Horse shared a tipi provided by Pawnee Killer's clan. They slept little that night, counseling over this new trouble.

"We have been bearded in our den," Touch the Sky said. "Whoever sent Goes Ahead under, he was able to slip past a tight ring of experienced Cheyenne sentries. What does this tell you, buck?"

"That he was an Indian, brother. A mountain Indian. A turncoat Ute, perhaps, or a Blackfoot."

"And if it was a Ute," Touch the Sky said, "he surely plays the dog for Bluecoat whiskey and tobacco."

"And thus, Shoots Left Handed is right. Soon comes the attack."

Touch the Sky nodded glumly. At this point, there was little they could do to prepare for an attack except pray and wait. The only hope lay in thwarting the whites disguised as Indian raiders. But could they move in time to prevent the annihilation of Shoots Left Handed's camp?

The first opportunity to try presented itself soon after sunrise the next morning.

The two visitors to the north country were counseling with Pawnee Killer and White Plume when a sentry raised a shout. He was hidden in the rimrock of the ridge which sheltered the camp from view below. From his position he could see all the way to Fort Randall and beyond, to the Milk River.

"Other sentries, far across the river valley, are in touch with him with mirror signals," Pawnee Killer explained. The battle leader squinted as he spoke these words, watching carefully as the sentry above now used his fragment of mirror to transmit the message to the main camp.

Pawnee Killer finally nodded. "As I thought. Our 'Cheyenne' raiders have been sighted again!"

"Where?" Touch the Sky demanded.

"There is a white way station on the Milk River Road, near Roaring Horse Creek. The wagons and coaches always stop here to water their horses. It would seem our pretend Cheyennes— five of them, as always—are lurking in a coulee nearby, waiting to strike when that happens."

"Five of them," Little Horse said. "Could we not form a war party and ride hard, and perhaps stop them?"

"I understand you are keen for them," Pawnee Killer said. "So are we, buck. But only think on this thing. How would a war party get from here to there without being spotted by whoever killed Goes Ahead? Even now, Bluecoats are closing in on our camp. We are no longer free to move in this area."

Touch the Sky nodded, his lips set in a straight, determined slit. "I have ears for this. A war party is no good. But two riders might stand a chance. Arrow Keeper did not send me here only to pray. Little Horse and I will ride out."

"Now goddamnit, Lumpy, remember. Don't talk so much. Just point your iron and grunt a lot. You're an Indian, not a damn jaw-jacking Frenchman."

Woodrow Denton looked at the rest of his men, checking their disguises.

"You, Noonan! Get rid of that damn quid, Indians don't chew. And you, Bell. Put some more of that berry juice on your face, you look like a spotted owl."

Denton, his four men, and Captain Seth Carlson sat their horses just inside the entrance of a deep coulee located a stone's throw from the Milk River Road. They had been waiting for hours. From here, they could see the approaching road and the way station built beside Roaring Horse Creek. It was a split-pine building surrounded by dilapidated outbuildings and a stone watering trough.

"Now remember," Carlson said, "they'll be looking for trouble. The freight company has hired two extra guards. They're riding in the coach with the passengers. Get the drop on them *after* they get out to stretch their legs. I'll be waiting back here in case there's any trouble."

A thin line of nervous perspiration dotted Carlson's upper lip. This holdup today would be even more lucrative than usual: The coach was carrying a cash shipment intended for the trading post at Pike's Fork. Now that Colonel Lofley was breathing fire to kill those "Cheyenne" attackers, Carlson knew this sweet little gold mine was almost played out. These last few strikes, with luck, might make his fortune, or at least guarantee an easy retirement.

"Shh," Lumpy said suddenly, cocking his head to listen. His tobacco-stained fingers probed at the goiter on the side of his neck. "Hear that?"

Soon the others did—the distant and steady jangle of approaching traces.

"Here she comes," Denton said, pulling a feathered bonnet on over his bald white pate. "Gotta die sometime, boys. Let's put at the sonsabitches!"

Pawnee Killer had quickly made a picture in the dirt for the two Powder River Cheyennes, showing them the country all around. Now, as their sister the sun tracked ever higher in a seamless blue sky, they discovered the merits of Arrow Keeper's ponies.

The country between the hidden camp and the Milk River Road was mostly a series of folded ridges. Heavily timbered, with few trails, they were a constant challenge to riders in a hurry. But Touch the Sky's blood bay and Little Horse's ginger buckskin seemed to sense, in the urgent pressure of their riders' calves and knees, the need to fly on the wind.

They strode the ridges almost as effortlessly as if they were open plains, racing at breakneck speed into seemingly unbroken walls of timber, yet always somehow sensing an opening. Their endurance, even for Cheyenne ponies, made the two riders exchange dumbfounded glances and foolish grins despite the danger they rode toward. How could any pony climb ridge after ridge, leap streamlet after streamlet, and not even spray foam on its rider?

"There!" Little Horse said, pointing as they crested the final swayback ridge before Milk River and the wagon road which followed it.

"See them, brother? They are just now moving into position in the last line of trees near the white man's lodge."

"If those are Cheyennes, I am a Ponca. I have eyes for them, brother," Touch the Sky assured him. "Our ponies are keen for sport, let us give them warriors for riders! If we ride hard, we can arrive before the stagecoach and scald some dogs."

Their mounts laid back their ears and put on a final burst of speed. Quickly the two Cheyennes cleared the ridge and emerged onto the badly rutted wagon road. Riding the smoother ground just to either side, they raced toward the way station. Each brave had pulled his long arm from its scabbard, and now held it at the ready in one hand.

Touch the Sky spotted it first.

A brief glint of military brass, emerging from the opening of that coulee on their left. And even as he spotted it, his newly emerging shaman's sense told him it was too late.

He pulled hard on the blood's hackamore, turning her toward the coulee. A moment later he was staring straight into the shocked eyes of Seth Carlson.

Carlson, shaken to the core of his being by this completely unexpected appearance of his worst enemy, held fire for just a second. Then, before Hanchon could lower his Sharps and snap off a round, Carlson pointed his carbine dead-center on the tall Indian's torso and squeezed the trigger.

Only a heartbeat after Touch the Sky made the discovery, Little Horse too spotted the officer.

"Brother, leap!"

But it was too late to jump out of the way. Even as Carlson pressured the last fraction of trigger resistance, Little Horse lunged off his pony and into the path of his friend.

Touch the Sky felt his face drain cold when, with a sound like taut rawhide bursting, the bullet struck Little Horse in the chest.

Chapter Six

"Little brothers! I have a thing I would speak to you."

Wolf Who Hunts Smiling allowed a rare note of cordiality to seep into his tone. It was his responsibility to train a group of the junior warriors in the arts of combat, tracking, and survival. Now his young charges were gathered about him while their tired ponies drank their fill from a nearby stream. A hard day of training was ending, and Sister Sun was a ruddy glow behind the Bighorn Mountains.

"You have done well today! You, Bright Hawk! Five times you aimed your throwing ax at a cottonwood while at full speed on your pony. And five times you sank the blade deep into hard wood!

"You, Two Twists! You launched fifteen arrows

in the time it might have cost a hair-mouth soldier to reload his carbine. And they flew straight, stout buck!"

Neither of the young braves thanked Wolf Who Hunts Smiling for this praise. Nor did they show gratitude or pride in their faces. They only held them stern, as the blooded warriors did around women and children.

Unlike Bright Hawk, however, Two Twists was suspicious. He respected Wolf Who Hunts Smiling as a warrior—only a fool would not. But any time the fierce brave became amiable, currying favor like this from the more popular junior warriors, it usually meant he had treachery firmly by the tail. Treachery involving Touch the Sky. Two Twists had only 14 winters behind him. But his brain was as quick as his bow. He saw clearly enough that Wolf Who Hunts Smiling was ravenous for power. And like two grizzlies circling before a savage territorial battle, Touch the Sky and Wolf Who Hunts Smiling were destined to clash.

"Little brothers," Wolf Who Hunts Smiling continued now, "you are doing your task as demanded by our Cheyenne Law Ways. But only think! Does everyone in the tribe respect the Law Ways? Do Touch the Sky and Little Horse? Does Arrow Keeper?

"I ask this, bucks, because it is common knowledge now that the old shaman sent these two riders out without benefit of Council. These two riders who have been seen counseling with white soldiers! I speak straight-arrow. Ask River of Winds. *He* saw them, and does he ever speak more than one way to any man?"

Two Twists felt heat rising into his face. He had to bite his tongue to keep from demanding: "And what of *you*, Wolf Who Hunts Smiling, who bribes old grandmothers into 'visions' against Touch the Sky?" But he tried to control his anger as warriors must. Touch the Sky had sworn him to secrecy about Two Twists' mission to watch Honey Eater. It was not wise to call attention to himself. But deep in his heart of hearts, Two Twists considered Touch the Sky the best and bravest Cheyenne warrior he had ever known. He would readily follow him into the very jaws of the Wendigo himself.

"Young brothers, only think. The wily old shaman can break our law, this Touch the Sky can break our law, even play the big Indian for the white dogs. But can you break any laws? Bucks, tell me. If you pull off an unmarried girl's rope, what happens?"

An uncomfortable silence greeted this remark. Wolf Who Hunts Smiling was referring to the knotted-rope chastity belt worn by all unmarried Cheyenne girls. Every young buck present knew full well the serious consequences of touching a girl's rope. The Bull Whip soldiers would beat them senseless; all their goods would be destroyed, their tipis would be shredded, their horses would be for those who took them; they could never again smoke from the common pipe or touch any common eating utensil.

"Your silence answers me well, bucks. You

know what happens when *you* break the law. But the doting old shaman and his white men's spies—they hold themselves above our Cheyenne Way. Remember this because *you* are the future of our tribe. Soon you may have to make a decision about which leaders to follow. Place my words in your sash and study them later."

Wolf Who Hunts Smiling fell silent. But his final words left Two Twists' heart stomping against his ribs. Clearly, something ominous was afoot! Often Wolf Who Hunts Smiling spoke with open admiration of Roman Nose and other young leaders of the Dog Men—the rebellious young Southern Cheyenne braves who had broken from the rest of the tribe which still followed the older chiefs and the Council of Forty.

It was as plain as blood in snow, Two Twists realized now. Wolf Who Hunts Smiling planned to eventually defy the established leaders and take over the tribe and its destiny. And now, somehow, some way, he was moving to eliminate the one man he sensed could stop him: Touch the Sky.

Two Twists knew he had to watch this thing closely. For a moment his eyes met those of Wolf Who Hunts Smiling.

I praised you publicly, but I know you play the dog for him, the older brave's mocking gaze seemed to say. *I may praise you to your face, double-braid, but watch your back-trail!*

While Wolf Who Hunts Smiling did his part to destroy Touch the Sky's standing with the tribe, Black Elk was back in camp doing his.

Like his younger cousin, Black Elk was a member of the Cheyenne military society known as the Bull Whips. It was their job to punish certain offenses and to police the tribe during ceremonies and the all-important buffalo hunts. They were quick to resort to their knotted-thong whips, and thus feared and despised by most of the tribe.

Now, as grainy darkness took over the camp and the clan fires sprang up, Black Elk stopped by the Bull Whip lodge. It was a smaller version of the main council lodge: elkskins and buffalo hides stretched over a bent-willow frame. From a pole in the front fluttered brightly dyed strands from enemy scalps.

Bull Whips filled the interior, smoking in little groups, gambling, discussing the news from the other soldier troops. Black Elk's keen black eyes searched out two of his favorite troop brothers.

"Stone Jaw! Angry Bull! One of my meat racks has collapsed. Come help me repair it."

The two braves, their highly feared whips tucked into their clouts, followed him across camp toward his tipi. They knew full well that Black Elk needed no help repairing a meat rack. But it was their usual excuse to counsel in private behind his tipi.

"Brothers," Black Elk said as soon as they were safely out of sight of the rest. "Do you think it might be time to replenish our troop's pony herd?"

Neither of his companions was noted for brains. They both stared at him in confusion.

"But Black Elk," Stone Jaw said, "the Bull Whip string has never looked finer."

"You yourself said so when Red Feather rode in with two more fine buckskins," Angry Bull added.

"You can never have too many fine ponies," Black Elk said impatiently. "The scouts report fine-looking mustang herds near the Valley of the Greasy Grass."

He paused, turning to look behind him toward his tipi. Like the others, it glowed dull orange from the fire within. He could make out the long, distorted dark line of Honey Eater's shadow. But he couldn't tell if she was listening or not. He lowered his voice.

"Have ears, brothers. Bluecoats are on maneuvers near the Valley of the Greasy Grass. If you were to ride in that direction, merely to scout the herds, you would of course have to be careful of the soldiers. And of course . . ."

Black Elk paused, adding emphasis to his next words. "If you happened to see the soldiers counseling with two Cheyennes, clearly you would be required to report this thing."

Stone Jaw was still lost, the puzzled furrow between his eyebrows deep. But Angry Bull had caught Black Elk's drift.

"Touch the Sky and Little Horse," he said. "No one knows where they are."

Black Elk nodded, letting this sink in. He had selected these two because they were among Touch the Sky's worst enemies in the camp. From the beginning, when he was first captured, they had argued for his death as a spy. Instead, the tall young stranger had won more and more respect within the tribe—but as he had, the hatred of his enemies had intensified.

Stone Jaw avoided Angry Bull's eyes, knowing the two of them might laugh and infuriate Black Elk. It was common knowledge throughout the Bull Whip troop that his wife loved Touch the Sky and he her. In fact, most of the Whips assumed the tall youth was holding her in his blanket for love talk, perhaps even bulling her. Of course, nothing was said in front of Black Elk. Perhaps his squaw had put the antlers on him; nonetheless, he was no brave to fool with.

Still, it would be satisfying to finally put an end to this arrogant stranger who grew up wearing white man's shoes and now played the big Indian with Gray Thunder's tribe.

"As you say, brother," Angry Bull finally said. "Our string could use a few more good ponies. Stone Jaw and I must prepare for a ride to the Valley of the Greasy Grass. Who knows what we might see there?"

Black Elk thought a moment. Then he added, "Do not swear to seeing this thing. Arrow Keeper might then force you to repeat your oath on the Arrows. Instead, paint broad strokes with your words. Say you could not get close, say only that you saw two Cheyennes. One was tall, the other smaller."

Black Elk thought of something else. He smiled, then added, "Say too that one rode a blood bay, the other a ginger buckskin."

"Arrow Keeper's ponies?"

Black Elk nodded. He knew his younger cousin

was moving to directly challenge the old shaman. At first Black Elk has resisted this out of respect for Arrow Keeper. But as his hatred for Touch the Sky reached a white-hot intensity, Black Elk could read the sign clearly. It was Arrow Keeper who protected Touch the Sky. Therefore, Arrow Keeper's power and influence must be hamstrung.

"We will ride out as soon as the Council agrees to it," Angry Bull decided.

"They will agree to it quickly," Black Elk assured him. "I am not just a Bull Whip trooper, I am this tribe's war leader. That pretend Cheyenne has somehow led a charmed existence so far. But even Arrow Keeper's big medicine cannot come between him and a bullet forever."

Hot tears welled up in Honey Eater's eyes, zigzagging down her pronounced cheekbones and dripping into the robes covering the ground inside the tipi.

She had seen Black Elk and his fellow Bull Whips duck behind the tipi. And though she could not make out their exact words, the treacherous tone alone told her that Touch the Sky's trials and sufferings were far from over.

How long could it possibly last? How long? He had suffered more than she would have believed ten men could endure. And that was only the suffering she knew of—what about the trials he faced when away from camp, as he was now?

A thousand times over she had regretted her marriage to Black Elk, yet what could she have done? Touch the Sky had apparently deserted the tribe forever, her father had crossed over, and tribal law forced her to marry. If only, through all of Touch the Sky's suffering, she could have been beside him!

Yet . . . and yet, she told herself with a burst of desperate hope, was there not the song sung by the girls in their sewing lodge? Though it did not mention their names, it sang of their love. And in this song, their marriage finally came to pass.

But how, she scolded herself now, could she be pining away about marrying Touch the Sky when his very life was in danger? Her own husband, assisted by two of the lowest and meanest braves in the tribe, was even now playing the fox against him. Even if it meant her life—and it well might, given Black Elk's insane jealousy—she must somehow thwart this plot.

More tears welled in her eyes as she thought of the stone in front of Touch the Sky's tipi—the piece of smooth white marble he had placed there as a symbol of his love. When that stone melts, he had assured her, so too will my love for you. There was a time when, by custom, she would check that stone each night when he was away from camp. And always, she found it intact.

But no longer. Black Elk had caught her kneeling before it and come within a cat's whisker of killing her. Now she could only think about it.

Outside, the big, mean warrior called Angry Bull raised his voice in sudden laughter.

I must watch and listen, Honey Eater told herself again.

War Party

She had already made up her mind when Touch the Sky rescued her from the Comanches and Kiowas in Blanco Canyon: Their two lives were one now. And though she would be banished forever, she would kill her own husband before she let him kill Touch the Sky.

Chapter Seven

Not sure if Little Horse was dead or alive, Touch the Sky grabbed him even as he slumped from his pony.

His face crumpling under the effort, Touch the Sky managed to haul his friend over onto his pony with him. But by now Carlson had recovered his battle wits. His next round flew past Touch the Sky's ear with a hum like an angry hornet. He felt a sharp tug on his foxskin quiver as a third shot passed through it.

More shots rang out, further away, and Touch the Sky realized that the fake Cheyennes were opening fire on their quarry at the way station.

Balancing his friend awkwardly with one arm, Touch the Sky finally pointed his Sharps in his free arm and snapped off a round toward Carlson. The situation was desperate: His first priority was Little Horse. Touch the Sky owed his very life to his loyal friend. So long as there was a chance that the vital force still beat inside him, the first obligation was to get Little Horse to safety.

Touch the Sky knew this without thinking, the way a she-grizzly fights for her cubs. So he also knew that Carlson had to be stopped from pursuit. And since Touch the Sky couldn't guarantee a killing hit with a one-handed shot, that meant he must do something repugnant to a Cheyenne and aim for Carlson's horse.

He dropped the big cavalry sorrel with a shot to the chest. Touch the Sky had the satisfaction of watching his old nemesis plunge to the ground hard, his hat flying off like a can lid—the second time he had dropped him unceremoniously from horseback.

Carlson! Even as he raced back down the road, leading Little Horse's pony, he found it hard to believe. And yet, it also made perfect sense. Now the young brave understood why Cheyennes were being blamed for the attacks. Carlson was again waging his one-man campaign against the tribe he hated most.

Touch the Sky was concerned with finding a place to shelter as soon as possible. Now and then a gout of blood spurted from the ugly, puckered flesh of Little Horse's wound. It had to be stopped, and soon. Otherwise, Little Horse was dead—if he wasn't already.

Touch the Sky couldn't tell how the raid was going. The shooting behind him had finally stopped. He raced through a sharp dogleg bend in the road, then spotted a thick pine copse well back from the road. Making sure they were out of sight from the others, he nudged his pony off the trail.

Every moment counted now, and Touch the Sky's mouth was set in its grim, determined slit. His movements were fast, sure, efficient. First, he gently laid his friend down on a thick carpet of pine needles. At least the bleeding had slowed. Still not sure yet if Little Horse was dead or alive, he quickly hobbled their ponies out of sight from the road.

Finally, he returned to Little Horse's side and knelt down near him.

It was time to find out if his best friend still belonged to the living or had crossed over to the Land of Ghosts.

He held his face impassive. But Touch the Sky's lips trembled imperceptibly as he lay his ear on Little Horse's chest, less than a handsbreadth from the wound.

Nothing.

Just a cold, hard wall of dead muscle. His Cheyenne brother had kept his vow to protect Touch the Sky's life with his own.

Touch the Sky's next breath snagged in his throat. His face went sweaty and numb.

A moment later, he felt it: a faint pulse in Little Horse's chest, weak as a baby bird's.

Weak, but Little Horse still clung to life!

"This is *not* a good day to die, brother!" Touch the Sky whispered. "You have not yet bounced your son on your knee."

Now there was no tribal crisis, no danger to Touch the Sky—every effort of his being was directed at saving his friend. First he raced down to the nearby Milk River and filled his watertight legging sash. He returned and washed the wound carefully.

Now came the hard part: removing the slug and cauterizing the wound, a process Touch the Sky had learned from Old Knobby, the former mountain man. He took the flint and steel from his possibles bag and gathered kindling for a small fire. When he had it blazing, using old, dry wood to cut the smoke, he unsheathed his knife and heated the obsidian blade.

Probing carefully but quickly, using just the sharp point, he managed to locate the slug quickly. Little Horse flinched, but never regained consciousness, as Touch the Sky removed the .52-caliber carbine slug. Next he heated the entire side of his blade until it glowed. When, all at once, he pressed it against the wound, the stink of singed flesh assaulted Touch the Sky's nostrils. Little Horse jerked violently, arching his back like a bow. But he neither cried out nor regained awareness.

Finally, Touch the Sky packed the wound with gunpowder and balsam. Soft strips of willow bark served as a dressing.

Touch the Sky tensed, making sure there was a ball behind the loading gate of his Sharps, when he heard hooves pounding past on the road. Then he realized it was probably Carlson and his thieving "Indian" cohorts, fleeing with whatever booty they had stolen.

The situation was bleak, bordering on hopeless. Another attack would now be blamed on Cheyennes; Shoots Left Handed's band was on the verge of being annihilated; and Little Horse lay balanced on the feather edge between life and death.

And behind all of it, Seth Carlson. The same corrupt, vicious, Indian-hating officer who helped to ruin his life as Matthew Hanchon, who tried to destroy his white parents' livelihood.

He glanced at his friend and told himself he would have to move him soon. It wasn't safe here this close to a road. Yet moving him in this condition might well kill him even though the bullet was out.

One way or the other, it had to be done.

Touch the Sky said a brief prayer to Maiyun, the Good Supernatural. Then he went to fetch the ponies.

"Things went badly," Pawnee Killer reported to Chief Shoots Left Handed. "Very badly."

The battle leader craned his neck to read the signals being flashed to him from the sentry in the rimrock above. He, in turn, was in communication with another sentry in clear view of the Milk River Road.

"The raid was not prevented. A white man was wounded. The youth Little Horse appears to be dead. Touch the Sky was forced to flee with his body. They are nowhere in sight now."

Pawnee Killer fell silent. Goes Ahead's widow was still sewing her husband's moccasins for the final journey, and now this new trouble.

He met his chief's glance. Shoots Left Handed's milky eye stared blindly back.

"This Touch the Sky," Pawnee Killer said. "I like him well enough. He carries himself like a man and seems to talk one way only. But Father, was Arrow Keeper right to send him?"

"His medicine is said to be strong. You have heard the stories: how his medicine can summon insane white men from the forest, enraged grizzly bears from the mountains."

Pawnee Killer nodded. "I have heard the stories, yes. But I also have eyes to see. I see that only moments after Touch the Sky renewed the Arrows, Goes Ahead was found murdered. Then he rode off to stop a raid. Now, once again, we are blamed for the raid. And now his friend Little Horse is apparently dead. If this is strong medicine, I would be spared such magic."

Shoots Left Handed said nothing for a long while. His good eye gazed out past the series of swayback ridges, toward the snowy peaks of the Bear Paws.

"I know Arrow Keeper, buck. If *he* sent these two braves, they were the right ones to send. Sometimes, we must wait for the flames to abate before we may read the embers."

Pawnee Killer cast a troubled glance back toward the spot where an intruder had killed Goes Ahead.

"As you say, Father. But even now we may be

in the sights of Bluecoat rifles. Sometimes, when the flames abate, the destruction is so complete there is nothing left to read."

The journey back to Shoots Left Handed's high-altitude camp was an agony for Touch the Sky.

Eyes and ears constantly alert to attack, he nonetheless kept a close watch on Little Horse. Touch the Sky had lashed him tight to his pony with buffalo-hair ropes. But each jounce in the trail, each stumble by the pony, caused Touch the Sky to wince.

Attack now, by Piegans or hair-mouth soldiers or vigilantes, would surely be fatal. But they managed to traverse the long series of ridges without incident.

Little was said when Touch the Sky rode into camp with his fallen comrade. Though no one aimed accusing eyes or words at him, he knew they had serious doubts by now about his medicine. But Touch the Sky cared little right now about their doubts. His best friend lay dying, the victim of a bullet intended for *him*.

Two braves helped him move Little Horse into the tipi he shared with Touch the Sky. Then began the long vigil.

Touch the Sky knew the immediate problem was sustenance for Little Horse. He had lost much blood, nor was there any nourishment in the destitute camp. Yet he would quickly die without something to replenish his system.

That night, when another pony was slaughtered to feed the people, Touch the Sky asked for a little blood and a few of the bones. He cracked the bones open on a rock and dug out the nutritious marrow with the point of his knife. He boiled this and the blood together in a potion. Then, painstakingly, using a bit of buffalo horn as a spoon, he fed it to Little Horn in tiny sips. Though the brave remained unconscious, his swallowing reflex worked.

That night, as was the custom with serious illness or injury, Touch the Sky stayed wide awake and recited the ancient cure songs he had learned from Arrow Keeper. All night long, the wind howled like the Wendigo while hungry babes cried. Finally, as the first rose-colored trace of dawn painted the eastern sky, Little Horse's eyes snapped open.

There was a long silence while they looked at each other.

"Brother," Little Horse said in a weak but clear voice, "I think you have saved my life."

"I hope so, Cheyenne, for you have certainly saved mine before."

"The pretend Cheyennes?"

Touch the Sky shook his head. "They got away."

"And now that Bluecoat is back. This Seth Carlson. I was sure we faced him for the last time in Bighorn Falls."

Already, Little Horse's eyelids were drooping with the effort of speaking.

"Sleep, buck," Touch the Sky told him. "Sleep long. You will need your strength. The battle has not even begun."

Chapter Eight

"Just remember, Carlson. The shit rolls downhill. That's not my cherished personal philosophy, Captain. That's the way the Chain of Command works. If I get thumped on from above, I thump on those below me. And I assure you, I *am* being thumped on."

"Yes, sir."

"I don't believe it! Two raids, practically back to back. Carlson, I was willing to overlook your miserable conduct and proficiency reports from Fort Bates. I happen to know the man who commanded your regiment there. Bruce Harding is a good enough clerk. As a soldier, he isn't worth the powder it would take to blow him to hell."

"My sentiments too, sir. He—"

Colonel Orrin Lofley frowned, nervously fingering his red goatee. "I'm not finished, Carlson, you're out of line! As I was saying, I was willing to overlook all that. But two raids mounted by a small group of renegades, back to back, and what's your battle plan? Has your company even pulled up its picket pins yet?"

"It's posted in the morning report, sir. My company deploys at 0500 tomorrow."

"Don't give me the smart side of your tongue, Soldier Blue. I know damn good and well when you deploy. That's why I called you in here. Those special weapons I requisitioned have arrived from Fort Union. Your men can pick them up at the armory after you sign the receiving orders."

Carlson felt a smile tugging at his lips. Since Matthew Hanchon and his stocky little companion had obviously thrown in with Shoots Left Handed's band, that was good news indeed. Anything was good news if it increased the chances of killing Hanchon.

"Very good, sir. I'm sure they'll be an efficient addition to the unit."

"They damn well better be."

Lofley shut up before he embarrassed himself. But Carlson knew he was thinking about that fiasco with the Hunkpapas—the infamous operation where 25,000 rounds of ammunition scored five kills, all women and children.

Lofley was even more agitated than usual, Carlson noted. Thanks to the newspapers making merry at his expense, humiliation had become Colonel Lofley's constant companion. Lofley confirmed all this with his next remark.

"I can't even look my own wife in the eye, Carlson. Her lying there in bed, so sore from a redskin bullet she can't move. And what does the horseshit-for-brains chaplain give her as reading material to pass the time? The Bible? Hell, no! He gives her the newspapers, full of scathing articles written by cowardly little scribblers who have to squat to piss. Articles about the supposed buffoon she married!"

Hell, Carlson thought, even a blind hog will occasionally root up an acorn. Why can't the newspapers be right now and then?

But he wisely held his tongue while Lofley wrapped up his tirade. "We're just goddamn lucky nobody got killed this time. But the paper-collar newspaper boys are reminding everybody over and over just how many gold double eagles were heisted. Carlson, you've got a history of fighting Cheyennes. I know that some tribes in the Southwest have learned about currency from the Mexicans. But since when does the Cheyenne tribe suddenly place such a value on white man's gold?"

This question was uncomfortable and made heat rise into Carlson's face. He realized, again, that his little scheme was played out. Ironically, Lofley hadn't asked that question until he'd read it in the very newspapers he hated so passionately.

"That's a puzzler, sir, it is. But the Cheyenne is a wily Indian with no lack of brains. They've found some use for that gold."

"Speaking of wily Cheyennes. Did you send Rough Feather back out as I ordered?"

"Yes, sir. As soon as I had his map and crystal-clear directions. He's been ordered to watch the camp constantly. If they move, he's to blaze a trail and follow."

"I see you ordered the band to remain in garrison for the deployment instead of marching out with you. No music?"

"That's right, sir. No music, no bugles, no flags. Just weapons and ammunition, all packed on the men themselves. The lack of fanfare is to remind the men of the mountain company's single mission—to kill Indians."

Lofley thought about that, fingering his goatee some more. Then he approved it with a nod.

"I mean it, Carlson. Don't let this explode in our faces while the eyes of the entire goddamn country are on us. When you do reach this camp, do *not* take all damn day in a complicated West Point maneuver. The longer it drags on, the more chance for something to go wrong."

"Don't worry, sir," Carlson assured him. "Nothing *can* go wrong. It'll be fast, it'll be efficient, and I guarantee, there won't be any Cheyennes left to report to the reservation."

"But why did Arrow Keeper send just us?" Little Horse said. "Without boasting, brother, I can agree he sent two of the tribe's best warriors. And perhaps, with luck and skill, two good braves might indeed stop these make-believe Cheyenne raiders. But buck, from all the sign *we* have read, the jaws of a death trap are already closing on this camp. Two braves are merely two more to die with the others."

Late afternoon sunlight slanted through the

tipi's smoke hole and the open flap of the entrance. Little Horse still lay resting in his buffalo-fur sleeping robe. His voice, like his body, was still weak. But the crisis had passed, and once again the sturdy little warrior had eluded Death's black lance.

"I too have given much thought to this thing," Touch the Sky said. "Arrow Keeper has entered the frosted years, truly. But brother, his mind is as keen as the blade of my ax. He has a plan."

"I have never known him to be without one, surely. But what kind of plan? Brother, you have eyes to see! These Cheyennes have reached the end of their tether. There is no place left to run, nor are they strong enough to flee if they could."

Touch the Sky nodded. "I know, brother, I know. You think that perhaps this time Arrow Keeper made us wade in before he measured the depths? Perhaps. Even the wisest owl can fall from its tree. But I do not believe Arrow Keeper sent us merely to furnish targets for the Bluecoat bullets. This time I do not think our battle skills were foremost in his mind."

Little Horse's forehead wrinkled in curiosity. He studied his tall young friend closely. Little Horse was among the few in Gray Thunder's tribe who had noticed the mark buried past Touch the Sky's hairline: a mulberry-colored birthmark in the perfect shape of an arrowhead. The traditional mark of the warrior. But such a sign also marked vision seekers and those whose medicine was strong.

"You mean, brother," he said slowly, "you

think the hand of the Supernatural is in this thing?"

But Touch the Sky refused to talk of such things openly. At any rate, he thought, his own supposed magic had done precious little to help their desperate kinsmen.

"Leave it alone, brother," he told Little Horse. "I can see that you are tired and need to rest again. Get strong, buck, find your fighting fettle! You are no good to me sleeping in this tipi," he added fondly.

Little Horse yawned hard. "I will soon be fighting like five braves," he assured Touch the Sky, his eyelids already closing.

"I never saw you fight any other way," Touch the Sky said, though he knew his friend was asleep.

Touch the Sky too felt the same sense of helpless frustration Little Horse had expressed. For now he was limited to constant scouts around the perimeter of camp, checking for more infiltrators. He had already helped erect breastworks of pointed logs, lining them across the one vulnerable entrance. Rifle pits had been dug behind these. But rifle pits were almost a meaningless gesture because the tribe owned only a few rifles and ammunition was critically short.

He stepped outside into the bright sunshine. The air, this high up, was rarified and clear, and he could see the mountains of the Land of the Grandmother to the north. As he passed through camp, some of the others cast odd looks at him.

Their looks were not exactly unfriendly. The Cheyenne people were too hospitable for such barbarity to visitors of their own blood. But the nods that White Plume and Pawnee Killer exchanged—clearly they said, "This stranger, so far he is a good nurse. Fine, but this is squaw's work. He seems useful for nothing else. As for his supposed medicine—add *his* magic to a rope, and all you have is a rope."

But Touch the Sky only held his face impassive in the warrior way, keeping his feelings private inside him. Slowly, as he made his way carefully down the narrow access trail, the camp began to recede behind him.

The sun was at its warmest and lay against his skin like a friendly hand. The cool mountain wind lifted his long black locks, feathering them out behind him like wings. It felt good after the close confines of the tipi.

Nonetheless, Touch the Sky sensed danger.

He glanced to his right, toward a wide swale —a low, moist tract of ground—overgrown with small bushes.

A tickle moved up the bumps of his spine, as light as a scurrying insect. Light, but it spoke of much danger.

Death lurked there at this moment, waiting. Just as it had waited somewhere around here for Goes Ahead. He was sure of it now.

Feigning interest in a point further down the trail, Touch the Sky moved on past the swale.

The Ute scout named Rough Feather flattened himself into the damp ground when the tall Cheyenne youth stared toward his position.

He cannot possibly see me, the big Indian told himself. This huge depression was covered with thick bushes. He had taken extra care in selecting it—after all, he was returning to an area where he had already killed one brave. They were alerted to his presence now.

Rough Feather had made his report to Carlson at Fort Randall. Then he had returned here at once, following orders to watch the camp closely until Carlson's special Indian-killing regiment arrived and turned this tribe's history into smoke.

This tall young brave—his buckskin leggings and low elkskin moccasins marked him as a stranger to this territory. But stranger or no, they all died the same.

Rough Feather eased his knife from its sheath. Because they were tall with especially long arms for Indians, Utes were noted knife fighters. Their style was to stand back and madly slash at an opponent's arms and hands in a flurry of wild passes. Then they closed for one perfect killing thrust when their opponent was disoriented.

But when he next peered out from behind the bushes, a line of nervous sweat broke out on his upper lip.

A heartbeat ago the Cheyenne had been there. Now he was nowhere in sight.

Touch the Sky made himself virtually invisible. Sticking to natural depressions and isolated bits of ground cover, he circled well behind the dish-shaped area formed by the swale.

Safe behind a tangled deadfall, he gathered up a pile of fist-size rocks.

One by one, he sailed the rocks high into the air over the swale. Each one thunked to the ground with a crashing of bushes. He covered the entire swale methodically, until one of the rocks chunked into something besides the ground—something human or animal that grunted in pain.

Touch the Sky didn't hesitate. The element of surprise was vital, but useless unless you followed through on it immediately.

His knife clutched in his fist, he leaped toward the spot where his rock had landed. The spy was fast for such a big man. He eluded Touch the Sky's grasp at the last moment and fled from his hiding place.

Touch the Sky recognized his tribe immediately from the brave's massive size and distinctive beaded headband. The Ute had at least three inches and 20 pounds on him. But it was his speed that truly amazed the Cheyenne. At one moment he was the pursuer; the next, the Ute had whirled and turned into the attacker.

The ferocity and speed of the knife assault caught Touch the Sky completely off guard. White-hot wires of pain sliced into his hands and arms before it dawned on him—he was being slashed! Again, again, hot steel sliced into him with the sting of a rattler's fangs.

The Ute's arms flailed like a white man's windmill gone Wendigo, his blade glinting cruelly each time the sun caught it. Touch the Sky took cuts to his hands, arms, face, chest, stomach, all the time backing rapidly away. Ribbons of his blood ran into the ground.

The Ute's exertions left his breath whistling in his nostrils. Touch the Sky's foot hit a rock and he went down. With a snarl of triumph, the Ute leaped for the death cut.

Desperately, Touch the Sky tensed his back like a bow and rolled aside just in time. The Ute crashed hard to the ground.

Touch the Sky, his lips a straight, determined slit, closed for the kill. His blade sought for the spot between the fourth and fifth rib, as Black Elk had taught him—from there it was a straight thrust to the heart.

But this finishing blow wasn't needed. The Ute lay on his face, immobile except for fast twitches of his legs. When Touch the Sky flipped him over, he saw why. The turncoat Indian's knife had landed against a rock and turned against him, driving deep into warm vitals.

Though he had been slashed many times—each cut like fiery bites—Touch the Sky's injuries looked worse than they were. Few of the cuts had gone deep into tender meat. But as he stared at the dead Indian's Army-issue shirt and trousers, he realized the awful truth.

No scout would have stayed in this dangerous area this long after discovering the camp and killing Goes Ahead. It would be a scout's mission to immediately return and report the camp's position. This Ute had already done that. Touch the Sky was sure of it. His job now had been to keep a close eye on the tribe until the soldiers arrived.

How long now before they arrived? Surely not long. Touch the Sky knew they wouldn't be riding in under a white flag—nor would they brook surrender.

It would not, however, be a battle. Not against Shoots Left Handed's dispirited, ill-equipped warriors.

It would be a massacre.

Blood streaming freely from his many slashes, Touch the Sky headed back to report this latest piece of bad news.

Chapter Nine

"Niece, no one ever told you marriage was a tender hump steak. Your problem is that you are a dreamer. I knew you were your mother's child, Honey Eater, as soon as you took to tying white columbine in your hair. You must remember that Black Elk is a warrior, tempered to lead when the war cry sounds. It is not easy for such men to show the soft side or be patient with girls who sigh and dream."

"Well, are not other men brave warriors too? Yet do they cut off their wives' braids or accuse them of treachery because they cannot bear their child?"

"Other men?" Sharp Nosed Woman said, watching her niece closely. "Just place these words in your parfleche, niece. *All* men gawp about and make the love-talk when their blood is hot for the rut. In time, they are all alike. The blood cools, and so does the love-talk."

"All men?" Despite her sadness, Honey Eater smiled gently as she recalled stories her aunt had told. "What about Grins Plenty?"

A rare softness seeped into the older woman's eyes. Both women automatically made the cut-off sign, as one did when discussing the dead. She had lost her husband Grins Plenty in the same Pawnee raid which killed her sister, Honey Eater's mother, Singing Woman.

"There was a man with hot blood and love-talk to spare," Sharp Nosed Woman confided, lowering her voice a bit and bending over her beadwork closer to her niece. "Did I tell you how he . . ."

She caught herself, looking at Honey Eater's innocent, distracted face. "Oh, but you'll blush and play the coy one. Never mind, never mind."

The next moment the entrance flap of Sharp Nosed Woman's tipi was lifted aside, and young Two Twists was staring at them.

"Sisters, may I come in?" he said, stepping hurriedly inside even before he had permission. He looked at Honey Eater. "I have a thing to speak to you."

Sharp Nosed Woman inhaled a deep breath, preparing to interfere. This was highly improper. Two Twists did not even belong to their clan; he should have announced his presence from outside. And to ignore an older woman, speaking directly to a younger—one who was married at that!

Honey Eater's confusion was mirrored in her

face. She knew Two Twists was a friend of Touch the Sky's, that this visit must have something to do with him.

Two Twists watched the older woman's face closely and saw her objections. Quickly he spoke up before she could.

"Sharp Nosed Woman, please find a soft place in your heart and forgive an ill-mannered Cheyenne! The women in my clan have long praised your beadwork. And the men, they say all the time, 'This Sharp Nosed Woman, how is it that a woman this comely is not marrying again?' I did not mean to be rude. It is just that I have important words for Honey Eater's ears. For her ears alone," he added meaningfully. "And I must speak them quickly."

He didn't need to add what all three of them understood: *Before Black Elk catches me.*

Although she knew the youth was openly flattering her, Sharp Nosed Woman had smiled gratefully at his praise. She knew he was here to talk about Touch the Sky, and she did not approve. At the same time, she too had heard the young girls in their sewing lodge—singing over and over of the great love between her niece and this tall young stranger marked out for a hard destiny. And despite her flint-edged practicality, tears always blurred her eyes when she heard it.

"Honey Eater," she said reluctantly, "I think I shall step outside and cut some turnips."

This was a thinly veiled sign that she was offering to keep watch. Grateful, Honey Eater nodded.

"Be quick," Sharp Nosed Woman added. "You know how dangerous this could be."

The moment she was gone, Two Twists said, "Sister, I have checked for you. The stone is still there."

Instantly, the tight bubble of a sob rose from her chest into her throat. But Honey Eater held it back. With that one remark, she realized, he'd meant the white marble in front of Touch the Sky's tipi. This was Touch the Sky's way of letting her know for sure that Two Twists was on their side.

Now she had someone to speak this terrible grief too! It was as if a dam suddenly gave way inside her.

"Oh, what do you know of him?" she pleaded.

"He is sworn to secrecy about his mission, sister. What passes at his end of things, I cannot say. From the look of the weapons he and Little Horse packed out of camp, I fear they are riding into great danger once again. But this much I do know. Thanks to his enemies here at home, especially Wolf Who Hunt Smiling, some terrible new trouble awaits Touch the Sky when he returns."

This was the first time he had managed to be alone with her. He told her about everything he had seen and heard, including Wolf Who Hunts Smiling's rebellious speech to the young warriors during training.

"This hotheaded young brave has the hunger of ambition blazing in his eyes," Honey Eater said when Two Twists had finished speaking. "These things he said, they are meant to do more than ruin Touch the Sky."

"You have eyes to see, sister, and your father's fine brain. He plans to lift his lance in leadership before the entire Shayiena nation. And their mission, under him, will be to kill as many whites as possible. He despises Touch the Sky and any others who believe some whites are decent."

"As you suggest," Honey Eater said, "Wolf Who Hunts Smiling is not alone in his treachery. My own husband and others in the Bull Whip troop are also playing the fox."

She, in turn, explained Black Elk's recent meetings with his troop brothers Stone Jaw and Angry Bull.

"No braves to fool with," Two Twists said glumly. "Something unspeakable is about to happen."

Time was short, the situation critical. Hastily they agreed on the only plan they could. At the very first moment when the plan of Touch the Sky's enemies was clear, both Two Twists and Honey Eater would appeal directly to the Star Chamber for justice and a chance to tell all they knew.

The Star Chamber was the Cheyenne's court of last resort. It met in secret at the request of Chief Gray Thunder, the only non-member who knew which braves belonged to the Chamber. Their decisions could override the Council of Forty. But although any member of the tribe could petition them, it was extraordinary for them to grant the request.

Two Twists was about to slip outside again when the urgent voice of Sharp Nosed Woman drifted through the entrance:

"Maiyun help us now, here comes Black Elk, and he has blood in his eyes! Do not try to come out now, either of you! Do not move or make a sound. If he catches you in there together, we are all heading for a funeral scaffold."

Honey Eater met Two Twists' eyes, fear widening her own.

"Good day, Black Elk!" they heard Sharp Nosed Woman call out cheerfully.

"It *would* be a good day, woman, if my squaw knew where she lived! Is she here?"

"No, Black Elk, I have not seen her this day."

"Then why is her beadwork missing? Whenever she takes it with her, she always comes to your tipi."

"As you say, Cheyenne. But she is not here."

There was a long pause while Honey Eater felt her heart pounding in her ears.

Abruptly, Sharp Nosed Woman laughed.

"Well, go ahead then, Black Elk! If you do not trust a woman who is your own clan sister by marriage! By all means, look into my tipi. This good widow has nothing to hide. Maiyun grant that someday she may."

Another long pause. Two Twists, sweat beading on his forehead, gripped the bone handle of his knife.

"I have no time to stand here and chatter with women," Black Elk finally said. "Nor interest in peering inside your tipi. If you see my squaw, tell her she knows where her tipi is and what time her husband likes his meals!"

Seth Carlson's new mountain company set out promptly at 0500 hours, deployed in two long columns of 30 troopers each. The grim purpose of this mission was suggested by the fact that no officer wore his saber—sabers rattled in the dead of night, warning Indian sentries.

Following their Indian scouts, the unit deployed south from Fort Randall toward a remote spine of the Bear Paws. It was here, according to the map furnished by Rough Feather, that Shoots Left Handed's band had found scant shelter beneath a ridge.

And it was *here*, Carlson was sure, that he would again meet Matthew Hanchon.

But this time, history would not repeat itself.

True, he may well have killed Hanchon's sidekick, that squat little Cheyenne whose war cry could scare the bluing off a gun barrel. But that slug had been meant for Hanchon himself. The only God Carlson believed in was gold dust. Sometimes, though, he suspected Hanchon had some kind of divine protection. Well, he'd need it for this next encounter, all he could rustle up.

Carlson let his sergeant assume the lead. He dropped back to ride up and down the columns, inspecting men and equipment. At first glance, they seemed a motley and unmilitary crew. Army dress regulations were strict only for garrison duty—in the field, men were mainly on their own. Experienced campaigners had learned to wear old clothes into combat. As a result, only a few of Carlson's troopers wore the highly feared and despised blue coats—most wore coarse gray cotton shirts and straw hats they had purchased from the sutler.

Despite their ragtag appearance, however, they were formidable indeed.

Each man was a qualified sharpshooter with the new seven-shot carbines tucked into their saddle scabbards. Each man had faced action against Cherokees back East, or Apaches, Sioux, or other tribes out West. Each man packed everything he needed on his own person or on a horse—there were no cumbersome supply and ammo wagons to hold this unit up.

"Ulrich!" Carlson called out, riding up beside a freckle-faced corporal on a huge claybank. "Are you clear on the operation of that new gun?"

"Yes, sir. I'll make 'er sing like a preacher on Sunday!"

The packhorse behind Ulrich carried one of the recently patented guns invented by Richard Gatling, as well as several long belts of ammunition.

"I fired it, sir, back East at Fort Defiance. This was when they was still testin' it. She's a reg'lar honey of a weapon."

Trotting beside the packhorse, Carlson curiously eyed the ten-barreled Gatling.

"She spits out three hundred fifty rounds a minute, sir! It's hard to credit even after you see it with your own eyes. But she does."

Carlson's jaw slacked open. "Stretching the blanket a mite, aren't you?"

"It's God's own truth, Cap'n. And there was plans on paper for one that'll double that rate. You just set the gun on its tripod and connect that magazine hopper thing right there. The barrels crank in a circle around that stationary spindle. You just feed the rounds into the hopper 'n' give the enemy jip! Hell, Mr. Innun ain't even dreamed of this gun yet. Gunna be some mighty consternated red Arabs, once this pup starts barkin' at 'em."

Carlson thought again about Hanchon's companion leaping in front of that slug. Let him leap in front of 350 of them!

"Well, you'll get your chance soon enough to impress me with it," Carlson assured the trooper.

He fell back to the end of the column. Two packhorses had been allotted for hauling the second special weapon requisitioned by Lofley: muzzle-loading artillery rifles.

Carlson was more familiar with these weapons, having trained with them at West Point. There were three of them, Parrot muzzle-loaders with three-inch bores. Wing nuts held the detachable barrels to portable wooden tripods that folded for packing onto a horse. With a muzzle velocity of 1,000 feet a second, their range was an incredible 3,000 yards. They fired ten-pound charged artillery shells that burst near the ground in a lethal, destructive radius.

Carlson knew that Indians had some knowledge

of Bluecoat canister shot. But Gatling guns and artillery shells were strong bad medicine completely foreign to their experience. When the Cheyennes got a taste of this, they would begin to understand the white man's concept of Hell.

Two hours after sunset, just as they were set to picket for the night, a Ute scout named Scalp Dancer rode back from his forward position.

"Indian camp ahead," he said.

Silver moonlight glimmered like fox fire on the surrounding rocks and pinnacles. Carlson's tow eyebrows knit in confusion.

"Not a Cheyenne camp? According to the map, that's hours from here."

The Ute shook his head. "Piegan. Not a full camp, perhaps a hunt camp. Perhaps twenty braves."

Carlson looked annoyed. Blackfeet Indians were not in the battle plan.

"Can we get around them?"

Scalp Dancer shook his head. "It would be a full day's delay because of cliffs and rubble on both sides of them."

Carlson considered, glancing back once again toward the Gatling and the muzzle-loaders. This might be a perfect opportunity to hone the attack on the Cheyennes.

"Would gunfire be heard by Shoots Left Handed's band?"

The Ute shook his head. "Too many ridges between this camp and theirs."

Carlson turned to his sergeant. "Pass the word back quietly. Rig for battle and prepare to mount."

Quickly, conferring with Scalp Dancer, Carlson formed a plan. Holding their mounts to a walk, enforcing absolute silence, they advanced behind the Ute to within 100 yards of the camp. Every man hobbled his horse and then fanned out in a skirmish line, advancing from rock to rock, tree to tree. As agreed, Ulrich moved into position first, accompanied by a private who had been shown how to feed ammo into the Gatling gun while Ulrich cranked and aimed it.

Carlson supervised as Ulrich set the gun on its tripod atop a flat rock. Below, Carlson could make out the shadowy shapes of the Blackfeet as they moved in and out of the glow of small camp fires. Another two-man crew assembled the muzzle-loaders.

"You two fire first," Carlson ordered, speaking in a hushed whisper. "That'll set up illumination. Then Ulrich opens up."

The rest of the men, armed with carbines, formed a semicircle behind the Gatling and the artillery rifles.

There was a long silence while bullfrogs croaked and cicadas hummed. One of the Blackfeet coughed, another laughed.

"FIRE!" Carlson screamed.

There was a belching roar from one of the Parrots; then below, the night suddenly exploded. A second shell, a third, exploded with deadly accuracy, hurling bits of rock, ground, and Blackfeet to the four directions of the wind. In the incandescent glow of the explosions, Ulrich opened up with the Gatling.

He cranked the revolving barrels once around to check the action. Then bullets were whacking into the camp below as fast as the private could stuff them into the hopper.

Carlson stood there in mute shock, forgetting to even draw his revolver. Nor was it necessary. The destruction below could not have been more complete if a hundred men had opened fire with pistols.

Indians, caught flush in the Gatling fire, seemed to perform a grotesque dance in the moonlight as the slugs jerked and lifted them like rag puppets. Horses nickered piteously and collapsed, bullets stitching snake holes across their flanks. Another artillery shell exploded, obliterating the faces of four Indians. Caught flush in this lightning attack, the Indians did not return even one shot.

Carlson didn't believe it, but his watch wasn't lying. The "battle" was over in less than two minutes. A few Blackfeet still required a slug to the brain to finish them off. But not one had gotten away.

Elated, throat swelling with the effortless victory, Carlson reminded himself: This was a far cry from Orrin Lofley's debacle with the Hunkpapa Sioux. And it was a sweet foretaste of what was in store for Hanchon and the rest of the Cheyennes.

Chapter Ten

"Is this a wise thing, brother, riding out by yourself?" Little Horse said. "One more sleep and I will be strong enough to ride with you. Perhaps I could now."

Touch the Sky was stitching a tear in his moccasins with a bone awl and buffalo-sinew thread. He looked up at his friend. Little Horse was recovering from his wound, though he still moved stiffly and tired easily.

"You shall not ride today, buck, though I would feel easier if you could go," he admitted. "But brother, I must scout on my own. That Ute I killed—or rather, who fell on his own knife—I fear he was only waiting for soldiers. I know that Pawnee Killer has sent out scouts, but I am weary of doing nothing except wait for death to arrive."

Little Horse eyed his friend's many knife

slashes. They were crusted in dried blood. "From the look of you, death has already arrived and been repelled."

"As you say. But count on it, he will return, and soon."

"Brother," Little Horse said, "do you think these pretend Cheyennes might be Bluecoats in disguise? After all, the little eagle chief named Carlson was with them."

"I have wondered this same thing. But soldiers or no, count upon it—they are palefaces. Carlson despises all red men too strongly to ever join with any tribe."

"I have ears for this." Little Horse paused, then added carefully, "I also have eyes to see."

"And what do these eyes see, brother?"

"That you are worried about more than the fate of this camp. That your mind is on our own camp, and how it goes with Honey Eater."

"Those eyes of yours see well. But if you have eyes to see, then you also have eyes to sleep. Close them, brother. I am leaving now."

"Let me ride with you."

"Has Little Horse been visiting the Peyote Soldiers? You must rest."

"*Ya-toh-wa ipewa,*" Little Horse called behind him. "May the Holy Ones ride with you."

Touch the Sky sought out Pawnee Killer and explained to the battle leader that he was riding forward to scout. Pawnee Killer, busy counseling with White Plume and Chief Shoots Left Handed, only nodded, his eyes sliding away from Touch the Sky's.

Again the youth realized: So far, with the exception of killing the Ute, he had done precious little to justify Arrow Keeper's faith in sending him. The others were only politely hiding their scorn.

Holding his face impassive, Touch the Sky grabbed a handful of the bay's mane and swung up onto his pony.

After the massacre at the Blackfoot camp, Seth Carlson ordered his men to make a camp for the night. The horses were still nervous from the sudden commotion of battle, the men still adrenaline-tense from the encounter.

Carlson set up the picket outposts, warning the sentries to keep an eye open for the Ute scout Rough Feather. He was supposed to rendezvous with the main unit, then guide them in to the Cheyenne camp.

By dawn, when Rough Feather still hadn't appeared, Carlson was fretting. Clearly, he told himself, something had gone wrong. Before he had more information, it was dangerous to move his unit further. Yet with Matthew Hanchon to sweeten this kill, this mission was too important to trust to the others. He decided to scout ahead on his own.

He ordered his men to lay low in a canyon sheltered from view overhead by huge limestone outcroppings. Then, after consulting the map Rough Feather had made for him, he broke out his compass. He sighted on a distant pinnacle and shot an azimuth. After he had his bearings firmly fixed, he set out.

* * *

Touch the Sky crossed ridge after ridge, sticking to cutbanks, coulees, and other natural shelters as much as possible. As he had been taught to do in dangerous situations, he did not let himself "think"—thinking distracted a brave and got him killed.

Instead, he attended only to the language of his senses. His shadow grew steadily longer behind him as he advanced north across the face of the rugged Bear Paws. Always, he was keenly alert for any sign of soldiers, watching for sudden movements by flocks of sparrow hawks and finches.

The provisions he and Little Horse had brought in their legging sashes were gone, much of it given to the hungry children. Now hunger gnawed steadily at the pit of his belly. It made him recall his vision quest to Medicine Lake and how starvation and murderous Pawnees had tracked him every step of the way. He had also had a brief glimpse of Seth Carlson, though his enemy hadn't spotted him.

He found a handful of chokecherries and ate them, popping them loudly between his strong white teeth. He was still scouring the area for food when he rounded a dogleg bend and encountered a huge deadfall.

It blocked the narrow trail completely. Sheer granite walls rose on either side. He realized there had to be a hidden opening in the deadfall because Shoots Left Handed's band had had to use this trail to reach their camp from this direction.

112

He approached, cautiously reaching out to separate the obstructing branches. Even as his fingers made first contact, a chill premonition of danger moved up his spine.

Carlson approached the huge deadfall carefully, telling himself the same thing Touch the Sky had: There must be a way through it. Rough Feather had marked some sort of obstruction on his map, but indicated nothing about an opening.

Carlson walked the entire length of the deadfall twice before he spotted it: a little opening, near one granite wall, that grew wider as one penetrated the mass of limbs and debris. Obviously it had been ingeniously designed by local Indians.

Carlson was a big man, with muscles heavily bunched around his back and shoulders. It was a hard struggle at first as he wriggled past the opening. But he quickly wormed his way through the leafy tunnel and stepped out on the other side.

Coming face to face with his enemy Matthew Hanchon!

The Cheyenne had been rattling the deadfall on the other side of the trail at the same time Carlson was emerging from his side. Each man's noise had covered the other's.

"You!" Carlson shouted, blood surging into his face. A moment later he was clawing at the snap on his holster.

Touch the Sky seized the throwing ax in his sash and whirled it even as Carlson's revolver cleared the holster. The officer leaped back just in the nick of time, the ax slicing past his face and missing by only inches. The leap threw him off balance, and he fell awkwardly into the dead brambles and limbs.

Touch the Sky's rifle and lance were back on his pony, well behind him. He raced at Carlson, jerking his knife from its sheath, and leaped on him as the big man struggled to stand back up.

Carlson was a trained wrestler. As soon as the Cheyenne landed on his back, he went forward with the motion, then tucked and rolled clear of his attacker. A moment later he had whirled and connected a solid right fist to Touch the Sky's jaw.

A bright orange light exploded inside the Indian's head. But he knew if he let himself pass out now, he'd never wake up again. Rallying strength he didn't even realize he had, he raced at Carlson full-bore and head-butted him, knocking the soldier back into the deadfall for a second time.

Before he could get clear of Carlson, however, the cavalry officer brought a vicious knee up into the Cheyenne's groin. As the Indian fell forward, pain knocking the breath from him, he latched onto Carlson's neck with both hands and squeezed with all his strength.

Carlson was pinned at an awkward angle, one arm trapped by a dead branch. His face bulged as the young brave squeezed harder and harder, then it turned purple, then black. The whole time, he beat at the Cheyenne's head with his free hand, adding bruises and cuts to the knife slashes already disfiguring him.

Touch the Sky refused to let go, his mouth a grim, determined slit. Finally, moments before Carlson would have passed out, the officer's twitching death agony dislodged a huge limb from the top of the deadfall. It crashed down on top of them, knocking the Cheyenne clear.

Touch the Sky wasn't hurt by the limb. But by the time he made it to his feet again, Carlson had his .44 in his fist.

The Cheyenne knew a moving target was diffi-cult to hit with a short-iron. He immediately burst back down the trail toward his pony and his rifle, zigzagging to make a difficult target.

Shots rang out behind him, bullets whanged past his ears. On the run, he snatched his rifle from its scabbard and then leaped for the side of the trail, even as another slug nipped at his heels.

For now it was a standoff. Carlson was crouched inside the deadfall, Touch the Sky in the bushes beside the trail. His pony was around a slight bend now, having shied back at the first shots. But he would be killed trying to mount and ride out. The Cheyenne had a rifle, which was a slight advantage.

Until he heard it: the sounds of more gunfire as Carlson's men answered his shots, letting him know they were on the way.

Touch the Sky hunkered down, snapping off a round now and then just to keep the soldier honest. But he knew he had to somehow get out of this death trap, and quick.

Concentrating on the sounds as men approached the other side of the deadfall, Touch the Sky failed to glance overhead. A sharpshooter from the unit had arrived ahead of the others and circled around through the rimrock. Now he was moving into position about 50 feet over the Cheyenne's head.

Only when the bolt of the soldier's carbine snicked home did Touch the Sky realize his danger. He glanced up, but too late. The soldier's finger had curled inside the trigger guard and was taking up the slack.

A second later there was a booming report, and the sharpshooter dropped dead from the rimrock, almost crushing Touch the Sky when he landed below.

"Brother!" Little Horse screamed, signaling from the rim of the opposite wall. He raised his shotgun to get his friend's attention. Some sixth sense had warned him to disobey his friend and follow him. "Fly like the wind now! I will cover you!"

With Little Horse's revolving-barrel, four-shot scattergun roaring over and over, forcing the soldiers to hunker down, Touch the Sky raced for his pony.

Chapter Eleven

"I don't get it," Lumpy said. "Wha'd'you mean, we ain't gunna meet up with Carlson after the heist? We always go to the shack and divvy up the swag with him."

Woodrow Denton was busy tucking horsehair braids under his Cheyenne headdress. He looked at Lumpy as if he were something he had just scraped off his boot.

"Is your brain any bigger 'n that bump on your neck? Now why would you *think* we won't be meeting him?"

"Cuz," said a man named Omensetter, "we ain't dealin' him in for this hand?"

All five of the disguised thieves sat their mounts in a little shortgrass clearing near the Milk River Road. Their rifles were balanced at the ready across the withers of their Indian ponies. By now the whites had gotten proficient at riding without saddles. Beaded leather shirts and fur leggings, the style of northern Indians, covered the skin that wasn't darkened with berry juice.

"Right as rain," Denton said. "We'll be going to the shack, but Carlson won't. Soldier Blue set this one up weeks ago. Since then he's got ice in his boots. His C.O. is still farting blood on account of how 'Injuns' aired out his wife. Carlson says no more Cheyenne attacks. But *I* say, he can go piss up a rope! There's going to be one more heist. This haul today will leave all of us in the Land of Milk and Honey."

"We talking gold?" Lumpy said.

"It will be soon enough. It's a freight wagon, and we're heisting the whole damned she-bang. It's loaded with good liquor, tobacco, and coffee, all bound for the sutler at Fort Randall."

"Hell," Lumpy said, "a wagon? Are you soft between your head handles? What need we got for such truck? We already smoke good Virginia 'baccy and drink top-shelf mash liquor. I reckon my coffee ain't fit for the Queen of England, but—"

"Lumpy," Denton cut in sarcastically, "if brains was horseshit, you'd have a clean corral, you know that? Of course *we* don't need the goods. The Blackfoot Indians need it. They need it so bad they're doing the Hurt Dance. Oh, do they want it."

"Blackfeet! *They* ain't got no gold."

"Neither does a beaver, numb-nuts. But what he don't carry in ready cash he's good for. The Blackfeet tribe is rich right now in good beaver plews. They'll give us every damn one of 'em for that wagonload of goods. Then we haul 'em to the trading post at Pike's Fork. The dandies in London are crying for their beaver hats. The price is up to two hundred dollars for a pressed pack of eighty furs."

"Hell, that shines fine by me," Omensetter said. "But the Blackfeet are no tribe to fool with. How do we get them plews without them gettin' our topknots?"

"I know a war chief named Sis-ki-dee. Leads his own band, palavers English real good. He's a crafty son-a-bitch and keeps one hand behind his back. But he's smart nuff to know when the wind's blowing something his way. I've dealt with him before."

"The hell we do with the freight wagon?" Omensetter said. "Where do we store the goods until we can swap 'em?"

"You ever knowed ol' Woody to leave any loose ends? I already checked behind the shack. There's a watershed gully runs right down to the road. She's bumpy, but not so steep a wagon couldn't make 'er. Carlson won't be coming around here for at least a few days. He's off in the field killing Cheyennes. We unload the stuff into the shack, then wait until nightfall and douse the wagon with kerosene. Nobody'll spot the smoke after dark."

"All right," Lumpy said. "But what about when Carlson comes back? Won't he get wind of this raid?"

"Does asparagus make your piss stink?" Denton

said. "Of course he'll get wind of it. He's a soldier, ain't he? But 'zacly what will he do about it? Go to law, for Christ sakes?"

Denton had been wanting to part trails with Carlson anyway. True, it had been useful having a soldier in his camp. But Denton realized this little piece of cake had finally gone stale. The newspapers were full of outraged editorials about the savage aboriginals. It was only a matter of time before the U.S. Army—treaty limitations be damned—sprang a nasty surprise on them.

So why cut the officer in on this last haul? Besides, Carlson wasn't putting all his cards on the table either. He was nursing some private grudge against the Cheyenne tribe. During that last raid, Denton had heard Carlson busting caps behind them, had heard riders. But when he'd asked him about it later, Carlson had lied. Denton had no desire to put his bacon in the fire just to help a man settle a private grudge.

Omensetter had broken cover to ride down and scout the road. Now he came racing back.

"She's a-comin'. I see a dust plume on the horizon."

Denton nodded. "Remember, this is our last strike in these parts. We're taking the entire team and wagon. That means no one can survive this one—they'll get too close a look at us and guess our game. That means we kill the driver and the guards. We'll leave the bodies behind with their hair raised and Cheyenne arrows in them."

*   *   *

Touch the Sky and Little Horse knew better than to flee south toward Shoots Left Handed's camp. That would be like leading wolves to a warren. Better to escape in the opposite direction, diverting the soldiers. Now that Carlson had recognized his archenemy, they knew he would lock onto their scent.

The two friends joined up while fleeing down the backside of a steep ridge. Arrow Keeper's surefooted ponies managed to find footholds that mules might have missed.

But Carlson's mountain troopers too rode excellent mounts—half-wild mustangs from the high country, broken in by Indian trainers. For some time they stayed right behind the fleeing Cheyennes.

And as they did, the two braves realized they were up against a dangerous new breed of Bluecoat fighter. Paleface soldiers were always dangerous down on the open plains, waging the style of warfare suited to their formations and training. But usually, in this kind of rough terrain, shaking white pursuers was a matter for Indian sport. But not now. Now they were forced to ride full out, barely outrunning the bullets behind them.

Several times they were forced to assume the defensive riding position invented by the Cheyenne tribe: They slid far forward, clinging to their ponies' neck with their legs. The rest of their bodies were tucked down under the horse's head, out of sight. If a pony were shot, this position allowed the Cheyenne to kick off and away from the falling weight.

"Brother!" Little Horse shouted as they raced along a rocky spine, looking for a way to cross to the next swayback ridge. He pointed down into a small valley to their right. "Look!"

Touch the Sky's glance followed his friend's finger. A moment later he tasted the bitter sting of bile rising in his throat.

Dead Blackfeet and horses lay sprawled everywhere, thick with blue-black swarms of flies. Touch the Sky, who had grown up next to Fort Bates, recognized the brass casings of artillery shells. His face went cold and numb when he saw that several of the bodies had literally been blown apart. Carrion birds were everywhere, forming a living, moving carpet of black over everything.

It took him a moment to realize why the birds kept turning their heads to expel something from their beaks. Then he understood. They were spitting out lead slugs—some of the bodies, incredibly, had been shot dozens of times.

The two braves locked glances. Little Horse was clearly dumbfounded—what kind of powerful hair-face magic could open a man up like a dressed-out deer?

But there was no time to wonder. Behind them, a sharpshooter's carbine cracked, and a bullet whizzed past so close to Touch the Sky's ear that it sounded like a bumblebee.

Despite the tenacious mustangs pursuing them, the superior training of Arrow Keeper's ponies eventually began to show. But as the distance between Carlson's men and them opened up, Touch the Sky saw that fatigue was sapping Little Horse.

"Brother!" he said. "Make for the wagon road. These ponies are keen for speed. It is dangerous to ride in the open, but we must open the distance and then you must rest."

His words rallied Little Horse. "I have ears for this. As you said when I lay in the tipi, brother. Today is not a good day to die! *Hi-ya, hii-ya!*"

Touch the Sky's hunch proved right. Arrow Keeper had indeed blessed these ponies with great speed.

Not since his great chase across the plains after Henri Lagace, the white whiskey trader, had Touch the Sky felt a pony fly on the wind as his blood bay did now. Nor did Little Horse's buckskin lack heart for the run. Once they gained the wagon road, both animals tucked their ears back and forced their riders to hang on dearly.

Carlson and his men were nowhere in sight. Touch the Sky's plan was to find a good shelter for Little Horse, then backtrack and find the soldiers. If they planned to resume the ride to Shoots Left Handed's village, Touch the Sky would have to somehow divert them—even if he had to make himself a target again for Carlson.

They flew over a rise, rounded an S-turn, then drew their mounts in when they saw what lay beside the road.

Three white men, riddled with bullets and arrows—flint-tipped Cheyenne arrows. All three had also been scalped. The attack had been recent, for the pungent smell of spent cordite still tainted the air.

"Our make-believe Cheyennes are back," Little Horse said.

"All the merrier for us," Touch the Sky replied, "if we are caught down here. Do not forget a Bluecoat pack is on our heels, buck! Now we ride."

But despite their urgency to escape, they were soon forced to stop once again, amazement starched into their faces.

The two young braves had left the road and were threading their way across a long pine slope. They were slipping across the treeless swath of a watershed when Touch the Sky spotted the danger just in time to halt his friend in the trees.

Well up the slope, the watershed veered hard right and disappeared behind the treeline. Just to the left of this point stood a run-down shack. A huge wooden wagon stood in the watershed nearby, wheels chocked with hunks of wood. Several men worked steadily at hauling goods from the wagon into the shack— men dressed in Cheyenne garb, though most had removed their fake braids and went bareheaded. One was bald as a newborn, another had an odd lump on his neck. All looked like hard-bitten killers. The two Indians could clearly make out where the white men had dyed their skin.

"Finally," Little Horse said, keeping his voice low, "we meet the white dogs who would stain our sacred Arrows. I am for them now, buck! I count five. We have killed more."

"We have, but not so many as are still closing in behind us, brother. And do not forget how close this place is to the soldiertown called Fort Randall. If you want to catch an eagle, you never climb up to its nest. Nor is this any place to be attacking hair-faces when you still lack red blood. Maiyun will be with us enough, buck, if we are alive tomorrow when Sister Sun claims the sky."

Little Horse frowned at these words at first, still keen to send their enemies under. Then, as weariness began to make his limbs feel like stones, he saw the truth of his friend's words.

"It is clear Arrow Keeper had a hand in shaping you," Little Horse said admiringly. "As you say, now we ride."

"As for these," Touch the Sky said, nodding up the slope. "I feel we may lock horns yet. For now, let us remember that Shoots Left Handed's camp is the next place Carlson will hope to find us."

"Then, brother, let us not disappoint so worthy a foe. Let us be there to welcome him!"

Chapter Twelve

While Touch the Sky and Little Horse were fighting for their lives up north in the Bear Paws, their enemies back at the Powder River camp continued to tighten the net of danger around them.

Even as the white thieves were loading stolen goods into the shack, the Headmen were meeting in council. The common pipe had been smoked and laid aside. Now the Headmen and warriors—the only ones permitted to attend at council—sat in a semicircle listening to an important report from the Bull Whips named Stone Jaw and Angry Bull. Though he was the youngest brave present, Two Twists was allowed to attend. This was in recognition of his bold fighting against the Kiowa and Comanche during the last buffalo hunt.

"Fathers and Brothers!" Angry Bull said. "You have heard me recite my coups. Now have ears for these words. Several sleeps ago, Lone Bear, leader of our Bull Whip troop, sent me and Stone Jaw to the Valley of the Greasy Grass. Our mission was to scout the wild pony herds. Our riding out was approved in council."

Black Elk had instructed Angry Bull to include this last sentence. Now Black Elk slyly watched Arrow Keeper. But the old shaman merely held his seamed face impassive, revealing nothing.

"When we arrived, we found paleface soldiers on maneuvers there. They were accompanied by turncoat Pawnee scouts. It was a mighty battle force."

Though this news made many uneasy, it drew few surprised reactions. The Valley of the Greasy Grass offered excellent graze and was a favorite spot for the hair-face war games.

"And we saw two Cheyennes counseling with them. Eating their contaminated food, drinking their strong water."

A shocked silence met this remark. Now Two Twists understood what was on the spit. A tight bubble of anger rose inside him.

"We dared not ride close enough to study them well," Angry Bull continued. "True it is, they might have come from any band. But one was tall, the other short and solid. They rode a blood bay and a ginger buckskin."

Everyone present knew by now that Touch the Sky and Little Horse were missing. Again, Two Twists watched all eyes focus on Arrow Keeper. Everyone present also knew those were his ponies. But his face was still an inscrutable leather mask.

Like Two Twists, Arrow Keeper read the sign clearly enough. Touch the Sky's enemies knew better than to swear they had recognized him—this could be verified by making them take an oath on the Medicine Arrows. Even the most corrupt Cheyenne feared such serious blasphemy. But so long as they fell short of swearing to their claim, they were immune to such a demand.

The council lodge had been buzzing ever since Angry Bull's announcement. Now Chief Gray Thunder folded his arms—the command for silence.

"Stone Jaw," Arrow Keeper said, cleverly directing his question to the more stupid of the two, "you both got close enough to make out a tall and a short Cheyenne?"

"Truly, Father, we did."

"And you also got close enough to make out a ginger buckskin and a blood bay?"

"As Angry Bull said, Father. All this was clear enough."

"Then tell me, Bull Whip, which Cheyenne rode the buckskin?"

Stone Jaw gaped stupidly, glancing toward Angry Bull for a clue.

"The tall one," Stone Jaw said.

"The short one," Angry Bull said at the same moment.

Arrow Keeper smiled, nodded, glanced at Gray Thunder. "Remember what you just heard."

Now Arrow Keeper directed himself toward the leader of the Bull Whips.

"Lone Bear, I have never seen your troop's pony string look finer. Why send scouts out now?"

Lone Bear shrugged, already well rehearsed by Black Elk and Wolf Who Hunts Smiling. When he answered, he used the new tone Wolf Who Hunts Smiling had assumed with Arrow Keeper—not one of respect, but of condescending amusement, as if Arrow Keeper were senile.

"Father, since when can Cheyennes have too many good ponies? This is truly an embarrassment of riches."

Several braves laughed at this. Now Wolf Who Hunts Smiling spoke up.

"Clearly, Arrow Keeper does not believe Angry Bull speaks straight-arrow. Our old shaman can resolve this mystery for us quickly enough. Where did he send Woman Fa—that is, Touch the Sky and Little Horse?"

Again all eyes were trained on Arrow Keeper. He could reveal the mission. But such information would alert Touch the Sky's enemies as to the direction from which he and Little Horse would return—assuming they survived their ordeal up north. Then they would face death as they rode in.

"It is a sorry day," Arrow Keeper announced, his voice solemn as he stared at Wolf Who Hunts Smiling, "when Cheyennes would conspire to stain the sacred Arrows by shedding the blood of their own."

Now he looked at Angry Bull. "You say we

should listen to you here today because you have recited your coups. True it is, you have counted coup. Do you think *he* has not? Who here now saw him count first coup at the Tongue River Battle, which saved our hunting grounds from the white land-grabbers?"

"I did, Father," said Tangle Hair, a Bowstring soldier.

"You and many others, buck! You and many others also saw him savagely beaten when *this* one"—Arrow Keeper nodded toward Wolf Who Hunts Smiling—"lied and accused him of chasing buffalo over a blind jump during the hunt. This same two-tongued Cheyenne who also bribed an old grandmother to lie about a vision, causing Touch the Sky to hang from a pole for hours."

Now Arrow Keeper's accusing stare also took in Black Elk, Swift Canoe, and Lone Bear.

"It is a sorry day," he repeated, "when Cheyennes speak in a wolf bark against their own. Have not the red men enough enemies from without? Do they need to kill each other? Now look here, how this Wolf Who Hunts Smiling pretends to swell up with 'righteous' anger. Do not let him place a lie over your eyes, Headmen—he is a base plotter, and has the putrid stink of the murderer on him!"

Now Arrow Keeper stood up, stiff kneecaps popping, and turned his back on the proceedings. A moment later he did something no brave present had ever seen him do—without conducting the usual prayer and the closing smoke, he clutched the long clay pipe to his chest and simply walked out.

War Party

* * *

As Arrow Keeper had wisely foreseen, his abrupt exit from the lodge completely disrupted the careful ritual of tribal law. Chief Gray Thunder was forced to immediately suspend the council without taking further action. Otherwise, the Headmen might have voted with their stones—sentencing Touch the Sky to death or banishment.

Two Twists was in a welter of nervous excitement. For the rest of the day he stayed within sight of Black Elk's tipi, impatiently waiting for the brave to leave. Finally, Black Elk selected his favorite pipe and strolled across the camp clearing to join his brothers at the Bull Whip lodge.

Trying to will himself invisible, Two Twists slipped up to the entrance flap of Black Elk's tipi.

"Honey Eater!" he called out. "I would speak with you!"

The words were barely spoken before the flap was lifted and a slim, pretty arm reached out to tug him inside. Honey Eater had been sick with worry ever since Black Elk returned from council, smiling smugly.

"Two Twists! I know it went hard for Touch the Sky," she greeted the young buck. "Has he been banished or . . . worse?"

"Nothing yet, sister. But it went hard for him indeed, and only Arrow Keeper's playing the fox has delayed a terrible fate. Now the time has come. Touch the Sky's enemies are keen for his vitals. Now I think it is time to approach Arrow Keeper about our Star Chamber plan."

She nodded, realizing it was true. Black Elk should be gone for some time. The greatest risk was getting caught entering or leaving Arrow Keeper's tipi. But by no means could *he* come *here*—not now.

"Let us go then," she said, taking Two Twists' hand for courage. "I am frightened, Two Twists. We must be careful. Black Elk will kill both of us if he finds out."

Thus alerted to Black Elk, they set out. Honey Eater was right that Black Elk would be gone for some time. What she failed to watch for was Swift Canoe's hawk eye. Black Elk, suspecting something, had instructed him to watch his tipi while he was gone. Now Swift Canoe saw Black Elk's wife and Two Twists slip out, hand in hand, and hurry across toward Arrow Keeper's tipi.

Now the bull will roar, Swift Canoe assured himself as he hurried off toward the Bull Whip lodge.

Arrow Keeper listened patiently, as still and quiet as the totems in front of the council lodge, while Two Twists summed up everything he had seen and heard.

"Away from camp, Wolf Who Hunts Smiling is sewing seeds of hatred in the younger warriors, Father. He speaks against you and the other elders, calling you soft-brained fools who play the dogs for hair-faces. He plans to take over the tribe. And because Touch the Sky is your loyal ally, Wolf Who Hunts Smiling is eager to kill him."

Two Twists fell silent. Now Honey Eater told about all she had seen—about Black Elk's plotting with Angry Bull and Stone Jaw before they rode out, as well as his secret meetings with Wolf Who Hunts Smiling and Swift Canoe.

When both had finished speaking, Arrow Keeper pulled his blanket tighter around his shoulders. Finally he spoke.

"Perhaps I may try to approach the Star Chamber. But this thing troubles me: that we have no proof, nothing we may offer them to place in their sashes. Rebellious speeches by Wolf Who Hunts Smiling, furtive meetings between Black Elk and his Bull Whip brothers, to the Star Chamber these are things of smoke.

"Remember, young ones. The Star Chamber is the Cheyenne's court of last resort. These are good men, but they are very reluctant to override the Council of Forty. If only we had some proof we could swear to. But we are up against some influential men in the tribe."

Honey Eater could not fight back the crystal dollops of teardrops running down her eyelashes.

"Father, my own husband is one of the murdering cowards who plans to do him in! I am worried enough about whatever trouble you sent him to face. Now I have to worry what new storm will engulf him when he returns."

"You and I both, little daughter. But the berry will not ripen before its time. For now you and

Two Twists must keep what you know close to your hearts. The three of us must stay silent and watch or listen for the proof we need. One solid word we may swear to on the Arrows. Meantime, give nothing away by word or glance, or I fear it may go hard for more than just Touch the Sky."

Grainy twilight had descended on camp by the time Two Twists and Honey Eater slipped out of Arrow Keeper's tipi.

The flap had no sooner settled behind them when strong arms encircled both of them. Hands were clamped over their mouths, and they were dragged roughly through the bushes and trees until they were well away from the main camp.

The two hapless victims could recognize their tormentors in the twilight: Black Elk, Wolf Who Hunts Smiling, Swift Canoe, Stone Jaw, Angry Bull, a few other Bull Whip soldiers.

Angry Bull held Two Twists against a tree, his mouth still covered, while Stone Jaw thumped his chest and stomach hard with his stone war club. Honey Eater winced, her screams cut off, as Two Twists flinched hard with each blow. Surely some ribs had been broken by now! But Two Twists defiantly kept the pain from rising into his face.

The Bull Whips formed a gauntlet, each trooper in turn passing by the tree and hitting or kicking Two Twists, striking him in the head with their bows, flailing him with their knotted-thong whips. When they had finished with their sport, Angry Bull turned him loose. Two Twists collapsed to the ground, breathing hard, bloody foam bubbling out of his nostrils.

"Report this to anyone," Black Elk declared, "and this is what we Bull Whips will say, to the last man: that we caught my squaw letting this youth bull her! Neither one of you will ever live with the tribe again."

But clearly, the main brunt of Black Elk's wrath was to be Honey Eater. Too late she realized he had overheard every word she spoke to Arrow Keeper.

"Brothers," Black Elk said to the rest, even as he pulled his whip from his sash and unwound it, "return to the lodge now. I have business alone with my woman."

The rest exchanged glances, nodding. This was right. This was Black Elk's business, to be settled privately. Swift Canoe dragging Two Twists, the rest disappeared into the gathering darkness.

"Now, you Cheyenne she-bitch," Black Elk said, drawing his whip back for the first lash, "the husband you called a 'murdering coward' will cool the blood that boils for your randy buck!"

His whip cracked, and Honey Eater felt an incredible pain as white-hot fire licked at her shoulders. Again, again, Black Elk's whip sang its lethal song. But not once, as her blood stained the earth and pain tensed her body like a bow, did the proud Honey Eater cry out or beg for mercy.

Chapter Thirteen

Touch the Sky had guessed correctly. So long as Seth Carlson thought there was the slightest chance of catching him and Little Horse, he would delay his advance toward Shoots Left Handed's camp. Now and then, as they topped a rise, they could glimpse the soldiers still dogging them.

But this game could not go on forever. The two Cheyennes were in unfamiliar country, an area swarming with blue-bloused enemies. And blessed with magic or no, their ponies would soon be played out. Nor did Little Horse possess the stamina for a sustained hard ride so soon after his wound. Already, the constant bouncing and jostling had started fresh bleeding. Eventually Carlson would hunt them down. Then he would return to his original mission of exterminating Shoots Left Handed's band.

"Brother," Touch the Sky said when they stopped briefly to water their ponies in the Milk River, "Arrow Keeper always says you must pop a blister before you can get rid of it. We have been running scared before a stampede. Now let us play turnabout and take the bulls by the horns."

Little Horse looked exhausted. A network of deep lines covered his face, and his normally copper-tinted skin was pale.

"How, brother? You saw that Blackfoot camp. These are some strong bulls on our tail."

Touch the Sky pointed toward a huge rock formation just across the river. Pawnee Killer had explained that it was a familiar landmark known to Indians as Wagon Mound because of its resemblance to the canvas-covered "bone shakers" white settlers traveled in.

"Pawnee Killer has a sentry up there. The same lookout who sent the mirror signals when the whites attacked. We are going to find him. Pawnee Killer said to let him be our mouth if we have messages."

"Find him? But why, brother?"

"Because it is time to play the fox, not the rabbit. Now hurry, while enough sun remains to send our message."

They forded the shallow river and pointed their bridles northeast toward Wagon Mound. While they rode, Touch the Sky explained his plan. The only map Carlson could possibly have, he explained, would be a crude pictograph done by that Ute scout. That meant distances and locations would not be precisely marked. Growing up all of his life next to Fort Bates, Matthew had learned this was one of the chief complaints officers had about their Indian scouts—the red man's vastly different notions of time and space.

Touch the Sky's plan was a strategy he recalled from the recent buffalo hunt in the Southwest. The two Cheyennes would indeed lead the soldiers to camp. But not to the camp of Shoots Left Handed—rather, to a false camp set up further down the trail. Clearly the murdering palefaces always attacked in the night, and with poor visibility it might not take much to fool them. Once the soldiers attacked it, the Cheyenne warriors would close in on them from behind. With luck, the element of surprise would counterbalance those terrifying Bluecoat weapons.

It was a desperate plan, full of risks, and both youths knew it. But at least it *was* a plan. As things stood now, they were simply waiting to die.

They reached the rock formation. After they signaled to him with the familiar owl hoot, the sentry popped up from behind a pile of scree and raised his lance in greeting.

They explained the urgent situation and their plan. Then the sentry, a brave named Eagle on His Journey, scaled up to the top of the rocks and broke out his fragment of mirror. Touch the Sky and Little Horse waited nervously below. If this message was not received, all hope was lost for the camp.

"They are signaling back!" Eagle on His Journey finally called down to them. "They will do as you say. They will meet you at the place you mentioned and bring the things you said."

Now both braves knew that time was their worst enemy. There was no way to double back toward the mountain hideout without Carlson and his unit knowing about it soon enough. They had to get well enough ahead of the soldiers again to leave time for setting up the camp and getting into position.

As they mounted again, Touch the Sky scattered some rich tobacco as an offering to the Four Directions.

Then he offered a brief prayer to Maiyun, the Good Supernatural, asking him to once again turn their ponies' feet into wings.

Their shadows gradually lengthening in the westering sun, the two Cheyennes deliberately rode straight into the teeth of their enemy.

Carlson spotted them as they emerged from a cutbank near the river, aiming due south into the Bear Paws. In classic Cheyenne style, they divided and raced wide around both flanks, also dividing Carlson's force.

And despite the superior training and breeding, these cavalry horses were also burdened with heavy ammunition and other field gear. As the chase once again began to lead upward, they began to tire more rapidly than the Indian ponies.

The sun dropped lower, became a dull orange ball just above the horizon. The trail wound ever upward, crossing steep cliffs and climbing torturously winding pinnacles.

"Brother!" Little Horse cried finally, "I see them ahead!"

The pathetic-looking group of underfed, discouraged braves waiting for them disheartened Touch the Sky and made his plan seem worthless and foolish. They had gathered just past a sharp turn in the trail, in a clearing under a ridge similar to the one further up where camp was located. There were only about 20 of them, only a few clutching rifles—beat-up British trade rifles, many of them held together with patches of buckskin.

"Brother," Little Horse said quietly as they drew close, "the children back in our camp could whip this group using just their toy bows and willow-branch shields."

"You speak the straight word, buck. However, no amount of hoping will turn them into Southern Cheyenne Dog Soldiers. So we had best work quickly and well. You shall soon hear enemy horses snorting behind you."

The braves had already started setting up the false camp. Several tipis were still going up, taking much longer to assemble than to take down. Fires had been built, and even two skinny nags—their ribs showing like barrel staves—had been tethered nearby in a patch of graze. Limbs and bushes had been stuck here and there to approximate human shapes. The size of the camp would not be immediately apparent in the darkness. Masses of bushes well back from the fires already appeared to be more tipis.

Touch the Sky stepped back for a critical

glance. It was a hasty job, but it would have to do.

"You warriors," he said. "The best opportunity for attack will not last long. You must seize it when it comes, and understand, it will not come twice. The moment the soldiers open their attack and move in, we must strike from the rear.

"You braves with rifles! One bullet, one enemy! We will have at most only a few heartbeats in which to act. That quick strike must be devastating enough to send them scattering. If they regroup, count upon it, you will experience a firestorm of bullets like you have never seen."

Down the trail, Little Horse was keeping watch. Now he called up to them. "Here they come, brothers, now the fight comes to us!"

"You know where to go and what to do," Pawnee Killer told his men. "The Arrows have been renewed, you are painted and dressed. If you must die, you are ready."

The Cheyennes knew that all talk had gone as far as talk could go. The rest now was in the doing. Silently, their faces grim, they moved back into the rocks and bushes circling the camp clearing.

Darkness fell, so black it seemed like vengeance. Yet Touch the Sky welcomed that blackness. Now the fake Cheyenne village took on a realistic appearance in the flickering, shadow-mottled light. The limbs and bushes did indeed appear to be vigilant Indians.

The fires burned lower as the night advanced. The soldiers, knowing full well the Indians knew they were coming, would expect the braves to be in rifle pits or behind breastworks in front of the tipis. The women and children would be expected to huddle inside the tipis. So Pawnee Killer had made sure his men built a line of log breastworks too, on which the enemy could concentrate their fire.

The soldiers waited well into the night, letting a damp chill settle over everything. Clearly they hoped to lull the Indians into thinking the attack would not come until tomorrow.

Touch the Sky had taken up a position behind a boulder just to the right of the trail. Little Horse hid to his left, Pawnee Killer to his right. When Little Horse imitated the clicks of a gecko lizard, Touch the Sky knew the sharp-eared brave must have heard signs of an advance. Sure enough, moments later Touch the Sky saw dark shapes massing toward them out of the night.

Touch the Sky had warned the others. Even so, when the first artillery rockets burst down onto the camp, many of the Cheyennes thought they were staring into the face of the Wendigo himself.

A tipi exploded, flaming bits of buffalo hide and wood flying everywhere. The explosion suddenly spilled a ghostly orange light over everything. The horses nickered in fright. Another explosion, another, and the ground seemed to be heaving all around Touch the Sky. Rock fragments rattled through the trees, sounding like a powerful hailstorm.

The Indians stared, fascinated in spite of their

bone-deep fear. What was this thing with a flaming tail so like a fire arrow? But no fire arrow could explode just above the ground like that in deadly bursts of powerful bad medicine.

A Gatling opened up, chattering its mad, lethal message of death. One of the horses was cut down, blood pumping from dozens of holes. Entire trees were fragmented as the bullets raked them.

Through all this, the Cheyennes held their discipline, waiting for the Bluecoat charge. It came only moments after the Gatling opened up.

Screaming their savage kill cry, the riflemen poured into camp to finish off the job.

"Hi-ya!" Touch the Sky screamed, *"Hii-ya!"*

Even before he realized how he had been duped, Seth Carlson had spotted uneasy signs. Why weren't the warriors singing their battle songs to rally their courage? Now, as his surprised men whirled to confront a rear assault, Carlson caught sight of his enemy Matthew Hanchon.

The officer was just in time to watch the Cheyenne squeeze back the trigger of his Sharps. A moment later, the soldier just to Carlson's left crumpled to the ground, his carbine flying from his hands.

Little Horse surged forward, adrenaline-quick despite his weakened state. His four-barreled scattergun roared and roared, dropping a soldier each time. In the precious few seconds before the soldiers could regroup, Pawnee Killer and other warriors also scored lethal shots and blows.

Panic swept through the paleface ranks like a

prairie fire in a windstorm. These were hard men accustomed to killing. But most of them were sharpshooters, experts who killed at a long distance from the safety of secure positions. They were not experienced in close combat, nor eager to confront Indians defending their very homes. After all, the soldiers were only in it for two hot meals a day and a straw mattress full of bedbugs back at Fort Randall.

"They've bamboozled us!" someone shouted. "We're surrounded!"

"Stand and hold, you white livers!" Carlson shouted, even as he drew a bead on Hanchon.

But a moment before Carlson's carbine fired, the Cheyenne leaped forward and used his tomahawk to kill a soldier who was about to plug Pawnee Killer from behind.

The attack had turned into a rout. Soldiers fled back down the trail, some abandoning their weapons. Ulrich was unhurt but unable to fire his Gatling because the private feeding ammo into the hopper had just caught a Cheyenne arrow flush through the eye. Watching the man flop on the ground like a fish out of water and screaming piteously, Ulrich had abruptly joined his comrades who were retreating at breakneck speed.

Suddenly Carlson too realized the danger he was in. Most of his unit was already gone. He was eager enough to confront Hanchon, all right, but only on his own terms. And being taken prisoner in a Cheyenne camp was no fate for a soldier— especially one who had already shed so much Cheyenne blood.

So far Hanchon had failed to spot him. Carlson decided to keep it that way, for now. But this was only a battle, not the war. Carlson knew that if he returned to Fort Randall without destroying these Cheyennes, his Army career was over. Worse, this campaign now was probably the last opportunity he'd ever have to kill Hanchon. And letting that red bastard live would canker at Carlson for the rest of his life, destroying the peace of his old age.

No. This tonight, he told himself again, would not be the end of it.

Clutching his rifle at a high port, he ran back down the trail and joined his panic-stricken unit.

Chapter Fourteen

Woodrow Denton's deal with the Blackfoot war chief Sis-ki-dee went off without a hitch.

Soon after the goods heisted from the freight wagon were stored inside the cabin, Sis-ki-dee and his braves showed up after dark with many travois piled high with beaver plews. The goods were exchanged, and now the shack was crowded with furs.

"Soon's we can lay hands on a wagon," Denton told his men, surveying the tall stacks of plews, "we'll haul the whole shitaree to Pike's Fork. Dragging them damned travois would be harder 'n snappin' snot off a fingernail."

"Hell," complained Lumpy, poking at his goiter, "why'n't we just use the damn freight wagon when we had it? It was plumb stupid to torch it."

Denton shook his bald, fish-belly-white head, clearly disgusted. Today the men wore their usual clothing. The "Cheyenne" raids had been pushed as far as they'd dared push them.

"Lumpy, what have you got inside that skull o' yourn? Rabbit turds? Did you swear-to-Jesus think we was gunna ease up to the trading post in a heisted wagon? One that's got 'Milk River Stage and Freighting Line' writ in big one-foot letters on the sides?"

From outside the shack, Omensetter's voice called, "Look sharp, fellahs! Somebody's comin'!"

"Shit," Denton said, suddenly all business. "You two," he said to Lumpy and the man named Noonan, "stay inside with the plews. Anybody comes through that door, you don't know their face—bust caps. You, Bell, come on out with me."

"It's Carlson!" Omensetter added.

"Worse luck!" Denton said. "The hell's he doing back so soon? He's spozed to be sendin' Injuns to the Happy Hunting Ground. If he's been to the fort and heard about that last raid, we can stand by for a blast."

Despite his bluff talk earlier, Denton feared Carlson's temper and didn't want him to know about that last strike just yet—not while this shack was full of plews. For one thing, Carlson would insist on dividing the profits up six ways himself—whereas Denton had plans to pull stakes and rabbit with the entire amount.

"All right," Denton said, changing his plan. "We'll all get the hell out of the shack now. We were just leaving, is all, after having us a little fun with a Mandan squaw, unnerstand? Let me do the talking."

Carlson had ridden about halfway up the watershed clearing when he spotted Denton and his gang, just now mounting. He hailed them, roweling his mount and riding quickly up to meet them.

"There you are!" he said, clearly impatient from searching for them. "I'm glad I found you, but what're you doing here? I told you not to come around here unless we had a job to pull."

His words secretly reassured Denton. The officer must not have heard about that last raid yet.

"Ahh, you know how it is, Soldier Blue." Denton winked. "Me 'n the boys here, we was just plantin' carrots in a little Mandan gal. She give all five of us a little fofaraw just for a half bottle of liquor. Too bad you wasn't here, coulda drained your snake."

Carlson wrinkled his face in disgust. The notoriously promiscuous Mandan women were known for being venereal-tainted. But obviously he had something more pressing on his mind than the morality of heathen women.

"The hell you doing in these parts?" Denton said. "I thought you was up in the Bear Paws giving grief to the red Arabs."

Irritation sparked in Carlson's eyes as Denton's remark forced him to relive the humiliating debacle of that raid on the false Cheyenne camp. Badly shaken, encumbered by wounded, his unit had deployed back to their field camp at the Milk River. The wounded had been transported back to Fort Randall. But Carlson refused to ride back through those gates himself until that Cheyenne camp—and now, Matthew Hanchon—were reduced to a bad memory.

There was one serious problem: manpower.

The botched assault had resulted in a dozen deaths and as many wounded in the Army ranks. The men were demoralized and nervous about returning to finish the job when the unit wasn't up to strength. But Carlson wasn't about to return to Fort Randall and request replacements. That meant also explaining how he'd ended up with a dozen men dead yet no enemy scalps.

"I want to hire all five of you," Carlson announced bluntly. "To help my unit kill Cheyennes. I'll pay you in good color. You know I'm good for the dust. You helped me earn it."

This took Denton by surprise, as did the sudden urgency of Carlson's tone. He had been about to laugh at the crazy suggestion. Now he thought better of it.

Why not? he thought. Why the hell not? Clearly Carlson had not been back to the fort and didn't want to return yet. The longer he put it off, the better for Denton. At least until that shack was empty again. Besides, this was a chance to make some more money while getting a little target practice in.

"Maybe. We talking rough weather ahead?" Denton asked.

"Only for the Cheyennes. For us, it'll be a turkey shoot."

"Well, if that's so, how's come you need us?"

"The more the merrier. I don't want to take any chances."

Denton studied the officer closely, noting the obsessed glaze to his eyes. This was a man on a personal vendetta. He wanted to kill some poor unlucky sonofabitch with a desire as intense as hell-thirst. He was so eager to kill him, in fact, that he was taking out insurance by adding mercenaries to his regulars.

Carlson pulled a fat chamois pouch out of his tunic. It was heavy with gold dust. "How about it? This one here's got brothers back in my quarters."

Denton stroked his chin, eyeing the gold. "What say, boys? Do we let daylight into some Innuns?"

One by one, they all nodded.

"Captain," Denton said, "'pears to me you just enlisted five more Injun killers!"

The victory over the paleface soldiers was sweet and heartened Shoots Left Handed's people. But the Cheyennes did not boast, as Indians do after a victory.

True, they had captured a few carbines and now had more rifles. But the false-camp ruse was only a way of adding a little length to the tether, not a decisive victory. The soldiers would be back, vengeance on their minds, and they would not fall for that trick again. Touch the Sky and Little Horse knew it as well as everyone else in the tribe. Next time the Bluecoat death company would know right where to attack, and the tipis wouldn't be empty.

Despite this grim truth, Touch the Sky's successful ploy had at least raised his status as a warrior in the eyes of the rest, if not as a shaman. Though they said little openly, Pawnee Killer, White Plume, Chief Shoots Left Handed, and the rest had decided that Arrow Keeper had picked a competent enough brave to send—only, the old man had erred in his judgment that the youth's medicine was strong.

Therefore, intent on preparing for the battle of their lives, most of them ignored Touch the Sky when they realized he was once again invoking magic to protect the tribe.

The decision had come to Touch the Sky while talking with Little Horse in their tipi. They had returned from the raid on the false camp and Touch the Sky had applied a fresh willow-bark dressing to his friend's wound.

"Brother," Little Horse said, "I saw Carlson's face during the attack. I swear by the sun and the earth I live on, it was like beholding the face of the Wendigo! He is crazy-by-thunder and lives to kill Cheyennes. Those guns that spit many bullets, the flaming arrows that explode—this power in the hands of such an insane hair-face frightens me."

"There is no place to run now, buck, and as you say, this Carlson lives and breathes to make sure we do not. This next attack, it will be the last one needed."

"We have renewed the Arrows," Little Horse said. "We have left our sacrifices. There is no more medicine to help us, brother."

But Touch the Sky was silent at this, recalling

something Arrow Keeper had told him once during a sojourn to Medicine Lake. There was a special prayer-offering ceremony which was seldom invoked because it was so grueling for the shaman. It was known as the Iron Shirt Song, and its medicine was said to be the most powerful that a shaman could conjure up. If successful, it could turn enemy bullets to sand or make them fly wide.

Tragically, however, the price of failure was the death of the shaman. And very seldom—almost never, Arrow Keeper insisted—did the ceremony succeed. And even when it did succeed, this could only happen after great suffering on the part of the medicine man.

But it had come down to this, finally, and Touch the Sky realized: *This* was why Arrow Keeper had sent him. It was the ultimate test of his faith in Cheyenne magic, in the Cheyenne High Holy Ones. It was the ultimate test of his belief in himself as a shaman.

As Arrow Keeper had wisely foretold, it would not be just his skills as a warrior which would save them this time—if they were to be saved at all.

"Brother," he said to Little Horse. "There is more medicine. But I tell you now, you will not like it. Do you have faith in me?"

"Will a she-grizzly fight hard for her cubs?"

"Good. You will need faith in me. Will you do what I tell you, no matter how hard your nature rebels against it? Will you swear this thing on your honor?"

Despite his confidence in his friend, Little

Horse hesitated before he finally nodded. This was serious business indeed. "I will, brother," he said. "I have seen the mark on you, and I believe."

"Good. Now hurry. The sentries at Milk River have flashed the warning. Carlson's unit has taken to the Bear Paws again. And this time he is accompanied by the white dogs who ruined our tribe's name."

Little Horse soon deeply regretted his promise to cooperate with Touch the Sky.

First, following Touch the Sky's instructions, they had gone to a remote spot just past camp in a thicket. There, Touch the Sky and Little Horse fashioned two poles out of saplings. The poles were extended between a pair of nearby tree forks, about a foot and a half above the ground.

Little Horse's face grew grim when Touch the Sky stretched himself between the poles, face down, and instructed his friend to lash his wrists and ankles to the poles securely.

His back arched like a bow, Touch the Sky said, "Good work, brother. Now, see that pile of rocks over there?"

Little Horse nodded.

"Start piling them on my back. I will tell you when to stop."

Little Horse hesitated, looking at him askance.

"Did you give your word or not?" Touch the Sky demanded. "Do as I say, buck!"

"Brother, this is—"

"Little Horse! If you love me as your brother,

you will not say another word. You will do as I tell you, and know you act for the people."

That settled it. One by one, Little Horse carried the rocks over and placed them on his friend's back. When Touch the Sky's breathing began to be forced, Little Horse stopped.

"More," Touch the Sky told him. "Keep piling them on."

The pain distorting Touch the Sky's face also twisted Little Horse's. Fighting back tears of pity and frustration, the game little warrior added rock after rock, until it seemed there was no place left to pile them.

He could not believe that his friend wasn't crushed by now. Each breath Touch the Sky took cost him an agony of effort. A group of children had spotted the strange spectacle and raced back to tell the adults. They just shook their heads, too worried about the upcoming attack to care about more supernatural foolishness. Secretly, some of the braves resented this young fool for weakening himself this way—he would be useless in the fight.

"Brother," Little Horse finally said, "I fear your back will break. Is that enough?"

Touch the Sky's words seemed to be spoken through several layers of thick cloth, the pain was so intense. "Are there more on that pile?" He could not lift his head now to look.

"There are, brother."

"Then pile them on, buck, pile them on!"

Chapter Fifteen

Carlson dropped back until he was riding abreast of the corporal named Ulrich.

"You've got a replacement on the Gatling? Someone to feed rounds into the hopper?"

"Yes, sir. Hank Jennings from the first squad. He's a mite soft in the brain, I reckon, but he keeps a cool head when it comes down to the nut-cuttin'. It wasn't easy, sir, finding a volunteer after what happened to ol' Smitty. Him catchin' a arrow flush in the eye like that, hell, the men figger it's bad luck on this gun."

"Yes, that was a bad break," Carlson said vaguely, his mind on nothing but the pleasure of killing Matthew Hanchon.

"Hell, like I tell the boys, sir. It wasn't the arrow in his eye what kilt ol' Smitty. It was when the sumbitch poked through into his brain!"

Ulrich slapped at his saddlehorn, laughing

again at his own wit. Carlson, the son of a wealthy Virginia plantation owner, detested the man, knowing he was from hardscrabble trash back in Missouri. But he forced himself to smile anyway.

"Good man. Make that gun hum, and maybe there'll be some sergeant's stripes in it for you. I promise, this next attack will be just like the raid on the Blackfoot camp."

Carlson had been forced to some tricky diplomacy since that defeat the other night. Morale was dangerously low at Fort Randall, due in large part to the poor leadership of Colonel Orrin Lofley. So Carlson had wisely avoided berating his men's cowardice in retreating as they had.

Instead, he'd appealed to their sense of pride as the Indian-killing elite. Every newspaper in the country, he assured them, would soon be singing the praises of the First Mountain Company. Wiping out that Cheyenne camp would restore law and order to these parts—and faith in the U.S. Army.

The addition of the five hard-bitten civilian riders had also heartened the men—especially when Carlson spread the false rumor that they had ridden with the famous Indian fighter "Big Bat" Pourrier. To this rumor the first sergeant added another: that the plug-ugly sonofabitch with the bump on his neck was a famous writer, one writing a book on heroes of the American frontier.

Now Carlson sensed it going through the ranks: a collective, fire-breathing will to give these upstart Cheyennes a comeuppance they'd never forget. Men who had bolted a few nights earlier were now determined to return with Cheyenne ears and skulls as war trophies for their grand children.

Now, symbolizing the tight esprit de corps of the entire unit, the sergeant belted out a training chant familiar to all of them:

> We're marching off for Sitting Bull,
> and *this* is the way we go . . . !

As one the entire unit responded:

> Forty miles a day
> on beans and hay
> in the Regular Army, *oh!*

Like a sinewy, many-headed death machine, the double columns wound their way steadily higher into the Bear Paw Mountains.

Little Horse refused to leave Touch the Sky's side during the grueling sacrifice. He was afraid his friend would suffocate, the heap of rocks finally crushing his lungs.

But staying with him, seeing this unbelievably painful suffering, was as hard as leaving him.

"Brother," he said at one point, "this has gone on long enough! Maiyun is stern, perhaps, but not cruel. He has heard your prayer by now. Now let me remove the rocks."

Touch the Sky only shook his head, too short of

air and strength to say anything. It felt like a huge stallion had plopped down on him. Each breath was a hard struggle and rattled in his throat like pebbles caught in a sluice gate. Otherwise, he might have told Little Horse that it was not a question of Maiyun hearing him—it was a question of deserving such powerful and direct attention from the Great Spirit that ruled infinity, not just Cheyennes. *A shaman must suffer*, Arrow Keeper had told him once, *to be deserving*.

While he waited, Little Horse tended to his battle rig. He cleaned and oiled his shotgun, and wiped every last grain of sand or speck of dirt off the few remaining shells. He pulled a whetstone from his possibles bag and sharpened the single edge of his knife. He used tightly stitched buckskin to reinforce a weak spot in his shield.

Throughout the squalid camp, the remaining braves were doing the same. Women, elders, children old enough to walk—all were armed with some kind of weapon, be it nothing but a pointed stick or a pouch filled with sharp rocks.

Pain was etched deep into Touch the Sky's face, adding ten winters in age. His tautly corded shoulder muscles strained against the incredible weight of the rocks. Surely his back must break at any moment!

But behind it all, Arrow Keeper's voice kept reminding him: The Iron Shirt magic was the most powerful medicine of all. A shaman, in contrast, was a mere speck of humanity. For those very reasons, the sacrifice to invoke the Iron Shirt protection must be almost superhuman.

War Party

As badly as he wanted this terrible pain to end, he must endure more for the sake of his people.

The sun was only a blushing afterthought on the western horizon. Carlson halted his men at the site of the first attack. The area was still covered with debris, mocking the soldiers' failure.

"We rest here," Carlson said. "We eat, we make our last equipment check. Then, well after dark, we make our final movement to the camp. Any questions?"

No one had any. Denton and his men stood in a little group to one side, mildly amused at all the attention they were getting. Denton figured it was funny as all hell, how all the soldiers kept making sure Lumpy knew how to spell their names—hell, Lumpy couldn't read or write his own name! But clearly they planned on impressing him with their killing power.

Carlson glanced overhead at the darkening dome of sky.

"Full moon tonight with plenty of stars. Moving in on them will be easy as rolling off a log. This time, count on it—you won't be shooting at sticks and bushes."

Well after dark, Little Horse's voice cut through the wall of red, burning pain. His words were calm, completely devoid of fear.

"Brother, the outlying sentry has sounded the wolf howl. Our enemy is upon us. Soon comes the attack. Now the rocks come off whether you will it or no."

At first Touch the Sky noticed no difference as his friend tossed the rocks away. Then, gradually, cramped muscles began to expand toward their normal shape. Little Horse knelt to untie the rawhide thongs which lashed his friend to the poles.

Touch the Sky's first attempts to rise to his feet were pathetic. Little Horse thought of a new foal trying to struggle up from the ground.

"Brother," Touch the Sky said finally, "I fear you will have to help me."

Little Horse had wanted to help his friend, desperately. But a warrior's pride was a delicate thing, and he knew it was better to let his friend try on his own first. Now, gently, he helped Touch the Sky to his feet. But still the brave could not straighten up completely nor walk except in a drunken shamble.

"Where are your weapons?" Touch the Sky asked him.

"I have given them to a brave who had none."

"But how will you fight?"

"I will not fight," Little Horse said.

Touch the Sky paused to look at him, waiting.

"I have heard," Little Horse said, "that an act of faith can sometimes give wings to a prayer. Sometime earlier, I heard you chanting the bullets-to-sand prayer. I know that you plan to stand where you will draw the first bullets. Brother, unarmed, I will stand beside you. If we are meant to live, we will live together. If we are meant to die, we will cross over together. I have spoken, and will brook no discussion from you. You are too weak to fight me, so accept it."

This was a long speech for Little Horse, and both braves knew it.

"All right, then," Touch the Sky said. "Then help me walk now, brother, for I confess I need your strength."

"You have it, Cheyenne."

Touch the Sky knew he must be a strange and disheartening sight to the others as he limped into camp, Little Horse supporting him. Already he could hear women sobbing from the tipis, many singing the death song and saying good-bye to their children.

Most of the men ignored them as they advanced forward of the breastworks and took up their position at the only approach to camp.

Another wolf howl sounded, this one much closer.

The Bluecoat death company was closing in.

It can't be true, Carlson told himself.

Again he cautiously eased his head around the huge boulder and glanced toward the camp, aglow in moonwash. But it was true.

Matthew Hanchon and his sidekick stood side by side, unarmed, presenting themselves as easy targets!

Carlson estimated the range. They were well out in front of the main camp, maybe only about 100 yards away. With his carbine, they were already dead.

He dropped back and spread the order: Nobody must shoot at the two bucks. Anybody else, but not them. They were his. Commence fire, he added, only when they heard him shoot.

Carlson returned to the boulder and laid his carbine across it to steady his aim. He centered the notched sight on Hanchon's bare chest and slipped his finger inside the trigger guard.

Breathe, he told himself.

Relax.

Aim.

Take up the slack.

Squeeeeeze . . .

His carbine cracked loudly, splitting the stillness of the night. Immediately, all hell was unleashed as his entire unit unleashed every bit of firepower they owned.

Even in all the earsplitting din, Carlson frowned.

Hanchon hadn't moved a muscle. But how could he have missed? He had qualified easily on targets up to 500 yards away.

The Gatling was chattering to his left, the artillery rifles belching smoke and fire to his right. Carbines cracked all around him. He could hear Denton's French bolt-action rifle making its solid reports.

Carlson drew another bead on Hanchon, fired, missed again.

He frowned.

A line of braves had surged forward from the tipis, and Ulrich raked the line with a sweeping pass of the Gatling. Behind the braves, tipis shredded, limbs broke, and objects lying about camp rolled and bounced as bullets struck them. But not one brave went down.

"Ulrich!" Carlson screamed. "You idiot, *aim!* You're burning good ammo!"

"Aim?" Ulrich shouted back. "Hell, I'm shootin' right into their bellies!"

Even as Carlson watched, an artillery shell thumped into a tipi. There was a terrible explosion, a shower of fire and sparks. But every occupant of the tipi ran out into the night, screaming and crying but completely unharmed.

Ulrich had seen it too. His eyes met Carlson's. Neither man was quite able yet to grasp exactly what was happening. But the first dull tickle of alarm moved up their spines.

"Keep firing that weapon!" Carlson growled. "Or I'll shoot you on the spot for mutiny!"

The braves of Shoots Left Handed's camp knew about Touch the Sky's special medicine ceremony. But none gave it any credence or even a second thought as the Bluecoats opened fire.

It was Pawnee Killer who first began to wonder why Touch the Sky and Little Horse were still standing.

Then, when he saw a limb exactly behind Touch the Sky suddenly snap as one of Carlson's bullets caught it, he realized—the bullet could not have hit that spot without passing through the Cheyenne. Yet there he stood, the worse for his ordeal, but clearly unwounded.

Screaming the war cry, Pawnee Killer led

his braves forward. Touch the Sky and Little Horse watched, their faces elated in the eerie flickering light of the flames and artillery explosions, as they washed over the first line of soldiers like a raging river obliterating a line of anthills.

Touch the Sky watched Pawnee Killer sink his lance deep into the soldier firing the Gatling. Other Bluecoats raised hideous death cries as Cheyenne blades and bullets found easy targets. Yet they could not score a kill against the Indians even at point-blank range.

One soldier drew his Bowie knife and lunged at White Plume. White Plume made no effort to move, yet a moment later the soldier's knife was embedded in the tree just to White Plume's left. Calmly, White Plume pulled the soldier's own pistol from his holster and killed him with it.

By now the entire camp knew that Touch the Sky's big magic had worked the ultimate miracle. Women and children raced forward from the burning tipis, snatching up guns, knives, hatchets. They rushed at the soldiers with open impunity.

A soldier held his gun to a little boy's head and fired. A moment later the boy smashed the soldier's cheekbone with a rock.

Carlson, his face a frozen mask of unbelieving shock, snatched up the Gatling from the dead Ulrich and set the tripod down so the gun was pointed directly at Touch the Sky and Little Horse. Hank Jennings had been killed, but not before he had stuffed the hopper full of bullets.

Carlson cranked the gun over and over, spraying a nonstop stream of lead at the two Cheyennes. He cut down an entire stand of cypress saplings behind them, but they still stood staring at him, their eyes mocking.

Only then did Carlson truly understand.

At first, like his men, he had been puzzled, then mystified.

Now, as Touch the Sky and Little Horse began to advance toward him, he felt something else: a cold, numbing panic that was building in his limbs and made the hair on the back of his neck stiffen.

He noticed it for the first time: The light in this village, it was unnatural, almost ghostly. A luminous white light, oddly different from moonlight, seemed to glow around Hanchon.

This place wasn't right.

He threw down the gun and bolted at the same time that Denton and his men reached the same conclusion. As those five tore off from the left flank, riding hard toward the trail, Touch the Sky cried to Little Horse, "Turn the gun for me, I can shoot it!"

Little Horse quickly did as told. Wincing at the incredible pain as he knelt, Touch the Sky led the five riders with his barrel, then cranked the Gatling into life. The entire tribe had the satisfaction of watching all five men fly from their mounts like clay targets lined up on a limb.

But even as the soldiers bolted in panic and a resounding cheer rose up from the camp behind him, Touch the Sky realized: Once again Seth Carlson had slinked away under cover of darkness.

Chapter Sixteen

To the vastly outnumbered red men, all victories against soldiers were sweet. But the remarkable triumph of Shoots' Left Handed's long-suffering Cheyennes had no comparison in the history of the Shaiyena people. Even before the battlefield had been picked clean, an elder had named this encounter the Ghost Battle, and the name stuck.

Word of Seth Carlson's ignominious defeat was not long in getting to the journalists. This topped Orrin Lofley's debacle with the Hunkpapa Sioux—at least Colonel Lofley's men had killed a few women and children. How, the writers screamed in derision, did a trained officer take such heavy losses without one confirmed kill?

The men's absurd story about Indian magic ruining their aim was only more proof of their drunken lack of discipline. The War Department stepped in quickly, immediately transferring Lofley and Carlson to the Dakota Territory and bringing in a new commander with a reputation for successfully negotiating with the red nations.

All this happened quickly, and Touch the Sky learned of it just as quickly from circular fliers and the newspaper published in Great Falls, copies of which scouts brought back from the trading post at Pike's Fork. The new changes gave Shoots Left Handed and his people the one valuable thing they needed: time. Time to get stronger and time to flee out of the mountains, back down onto the plains where this horse-loving, roaming band belonged.

The mass, panicked exodus of the soldiers had left a windfall of weapons and supplies for the tribe. The soldiers had been provisioned for quite a stay in the field, and most of their rations had been discarded in the rout. Now the tribe had hardtack, dried beans, bacon, coffee, and other goods.

Shoots Left Handed was able to wink at Pawnee Killer and the others. Had they not questioned his loyalty to Arrow Keeper, his steadfast belief that this Cheyenne youth possessed strong medicine indeed in spite of appearances?

"Already the babies have stopped crying and sleep through the night," the old chief told him several sleeps after the Ghost Battle. Even the eye covered by his milky cataract seemed to glimmer with new hope. "Soon the tribe will move south toward the Powder River hunting grounds, where we belong. The day of the red man has reached its final hours, and we must join one more time as a people before we follow the buffalo into the last hiding places."

Touch the Sky and Little Horse would gladly have stayed longer and traveled south with them. But as soon as he had recovered enough strength and movement to ride, Touch the Sky said his farewells. Trying not to worry about Honey Eater was useless. Her image seemed to be painted on the back of his eyelids.

The night before they rode out, they were feted as heroes and saviors of the tribe. But Touch the Sky found it embarrassing when several of the elders timidly approached and reached out cautiously to touch him, as if verifying he were solid flesh and bone. When he was asked to bless several objects with medicine, he politely refused, saying he was not yet a shaman.

"Brother," Pawnee Killer said as the two visitors mounted to ride out, "I confess that, at first, I was skeptical of you. Now I see that it was only unfortunate timing, this thing of finding Goes Ahead's body right after the Renewal. You are both straight-arrow Cheyennes and the finest warriors this battle chief has ever known."

"We will meet again at the annual dances," Touch the Sky told him. "Your ponies will be fat then, your camp full of dogs again as it should be."

Nearby, a group of children were throwing stones at birds. Now they shrieked with excited laughter when one of them nicked a finch and it flew angrily away.

"Brother," Pawnee Killer said, "I have not seen a sight like this for many sleeps. You are both warriors, so I will not embarrass you with too much gratitude. Just know this, and know it forever. It was *you* who gave those children back their lives. For this, I swear my own life to you. You have but to send word, and Pawnee Killer's lance will go up beside yours."

These words, spoken simply and from an impassive face, nonetheless swelled both braves' hearts with pride. But the final tribute came as they were about to round the bend that would cut them off from view of the camp.

"Brother!" Little Horse said, pointing back behind them. "Look!"

Touch the Sky did look. The children were playing another game. Two of them stood side by side while a group of them pretended to be soldiers, trying to shoot them with their stick rifles. The two unarmed children merely smiled smugly back as soldier after soldier threw down his rifle and fled in panic.

"They are refighting the Ghost Battle," Little Horse said. "I have a feeling it is going to be won many times over from this day on."

But despite the elation of this sweet victory, both youths knew they were riding back to an uncertain fate.

Their enemies had been conspiring against them even before they left; their secret departure from camp had only given their enemies more fuel for the fire. So they were not at all surprised by the hostile stares of many as they finally rode in, late one morning, and turned their ponies loose in the common corral.

"At least," Little Horse said as they crossed toward Arrow Keeper's tipi, "we were not arrested as we rode in. This means no decision was reached against us in council."

Touch the Sky barely heard his friend, so nervous was he about spotting Honey Eater again. So far he had seen no activity around Black Elk's tipi. At this time of the morning, she might well be visiting with her clan sisters.

Then he spotted Two Twists, and his face went cold.

The youth had been savagely beaten. He was leading his pony to the corral, obviously favoring his sore midsection. A mass of bruises covered half of his face.

His eyes met Touch the Sky's. Two Twists then glanced hurriedly around before crossing to greet his friend.

"Touch the Sky, I am glad to see you alive! But I fear you will not remain that way long around here. Your enemies are more determined than ever to—"

"Never mind that, little brother," Touch the Sky said grimly, still eyeing the bruises. "I know who did this to you. Tell me I am wrong."

Two Twists glanced at the ground, saying nothing.

"He will pay for hurting you, buck. But now

tell me this, for it is the only thing else I need to know. *Look* at me, Cheyenne!"

Two Twists did.

"Honey Eater?" was all Touch the Sky had to say. And the glint of confirmation in the youth's eyes was all he needed to see.

Vaguely, as if in a thick fog, Touch the Sky was aware of both Little Horse and Two Twists trying to stop him, trying to change his mind as he bore down on Black Elk's tipi. He felt them pulling on his arms, shook them off as easily as flies.

He reached the tipi, grabbed the entrance flap, threw it back.

Black Elk was gone. But Honey Eater was inside, brewing yarrow tea in a clay pot over the firepit.

Her eyes flew up, startled, when the flap was lifted. She expected to see Black Elk, back from his Bull Whip lodge.

Instead, the man she loved with all her heart stood staring at her—staring at the deep whiplash cuts in her face, on her neck and shoulders and back, clearly visible above the neck of her doeskin dress.

Touch the Sky said nothing. He met her eyes with his for several heartbeats. Then he lowered the flap and turned around, his mind bent toward one purpose only: finding Black Elk and killing him.

But it was Arrow Keeper who now stood in front of him, not his enemy.

"Listen to me, little brother, and place my words close to your heart. I know that you are now setting out on the course of murder. If you murder a fellow Cheyenne, the Arrows will be stained forever. You can never be a shaman with the blood of your own on your hands."

Touch the Sky shook his head. "Father, I swore an oath to Black Elk during the buffalo hunt in Comanche country. I told him, after he beat Honey Eater, that I would kill him if he touched her again. I swore this oath on my medicine bundle."

"And do you see *this* bundle?"

Arrow Keeper pulled a coyote-fur pouch out from under his blanket. "These are the sacred Arrows. I have hoped that someday soon, when I am gone to the Land Beyond the Sun, you would be the Keeper. Go kill this dog now, and you kill those hopes too. For you have made an oath on *this* bundle too, Cheyenne. An oath to keep them forever sweet and clean. Now make your choice."

With that the old shaman turned his back and walked to his tipi.

Miserable, Touch the Sky stood there, unsure what to do. Conflicting emotions warred inside his breast.

"Brother," Little Horse said in a low voice, "look behind you."

Touch the Sky did. Honey Eater had lifted the flap of the tipi and was watching him. Despite the cuts, her beauty again took his breath away.

And now, rising steadily louder, they all heard it: the young girls in their sewing lodge. They were singing the song about a Cheyenne girl and the noble brave who loved her—a song about suffering and patience and bravery and goodness triumphing over evil in the Life of the Little Day.

It was a song about *them*. And as Touch the Sky watched her, Honey Eater crossed her wrists over her heart: Cheyenne sign talk for love.

He crossed his too. And he understood what her eyes were begging him to do right now: She was begging him to make sure that satisfying his manly pride was worth being banished forever from the tribe. Because that also meant lifetime banishment from her.

He made up his mind. Speaking loudly enough for Honey Eater, Two Twists, Little Horse, and even old Arrow Keeper to hear him, Touch the Sky said, "Let us turn our ponies out to graze, brother, then bathe and sleep. It is good to be home!"

Judd Cole
Follow the adventures of Touch the Sky as he searches for a world he can call his own!

#5: Blood on the Plains. When one of Touch the Sky's white friends suddenly appears, he brings with him a murderous enemy—the rivermen who employ him are really greedy land-grabbers out to steal the Indian's hunting grounds. If the young brave cannot convince his tribe that they are in danger, the swindlers will soak the ground with innocent blood.

_3441-7 $3.50 US/$4.50 CAN

#6: Comanche Raid. When a band of Comanche attack Touch the Sky's tribe, the silence of the prairie is shattered by the cries of the dead and dying. If Touch the Sky and the Cheyenne braves can't fend off the vicious war party, they will be slaughtered like the mighty beasts of the plains.

_3478-6 $3.50 US/$4.50 CAN

#7: Comancheros. When a notorious slave trader captures their women and children, Touch the Sky and his brother warriors race to save them so their glorious past won't fade into a bleak and hopeless future.

_3496-4 $3.50 US/$4.50 CAN

LEISURE BOOKS
ATTN: Order Department
276 5th Avenue, New York, NY 10001

Please add $1.50 for shipping and handling for the first book and $.35 for each book thereafter. PA., N.Y.S. and N.Y.C. residents, please add appropriate sales tax. No cash, stamps, or C.O.D.s. All orders shipped within 6 weeks via postal service book rate. Canadian orders require $2.00 extra postage and must be paid in U.S. dollars through a U.S. banking facility.

Name_____

Address_____

City _____ State _____ Zip _____

I have enclosed $_____in payment for the checked book(s).
Payment <u>must</u> accompany all orders.☐ Please send a free catalog.

CHEYENNE

JUDD COLE

Born Indian, raised white, Touch the Sky swears he'll die a free man. Don't miss one exciting adventure as the young brave searches for a world he can call his own.

#1: Arrow Keeper.
__3312-7 $3.50 US/$4.50 CAN

#2: Death Chant.
__3337-2 $3.50 US/$4.50 CAN

#3: Renegade Justice.
__3385-2 $3.50 US/$4.50 CAN

#4: Vision Quest.
__3411-5 $3.50 US/$4.50 CAN